Mandie Mysteries

Mandie's Cookbook

MANDIE
AND THE
SINGING
CHALET

Lois Gladys Leppard

BETHANY HOUSE PUBLISHERS
MINNEAPOLIS, MINNESOTA 55438

Mandie and the Singing Chalet
Lois Gladys Leppard

Library of Congress Catalog Card Number 90-56206

ISBN 1-55661-198-6

Published by Bethany House Publishers
A Ministry of Bethany Fellowship, Inc.
6820 Auto Club Road, Minneapolis, Minnesota 55438

Printed in the United States of America

In memory of
my dear friend
and world-renowned opera star

Enricka Zaranova

of New York
whose last name I have borrowed
for this book.

About the Author

LOIS GLADYS LEPPARD has been a Federal Civil Service employee in various countries around the world. She makes her home in South Carolina.

The stories of her own mother's childhood are the basis for many of the incidents incorporated in this series.

Contents

He that despiseth his neighbor sinneth: but he that

hath mercy on the poor, happy is he.

Proverbs 14:21

Chapter 1 / Midnight in Switzerland

"Amanda! Wake up! We're at the Thalers'," Mrs. Taft said, as she gently shook her granddaughter's shoulder.

Mandie, comfortably resting in the corner of the carriage seat, blinked her blue eyes and straightened up. She looked out the window into the darkness, but could only see faint lights on an enormous doorway. Snowball, her white kitten, uncurled in her lap, then stretched and yawned.

"Oh, we're in Switzerland!" Mandie said excitedly to her friend, Celia Hamilton.

"Of course we're in Switzerland. Where did you think we were?" answered Celia, sitting next to her.

"I—I must have been dreaming," Mandie explained. "I was back home in Franklin, North Carolina, and my mother was rocking my baby brother to sleep."

"I hope you don't get homesick," fourteen-year-old

Jonathan Guyer teased, with a mischievous smile brightening his face.

Before Mandie could reply, her grandmother stood up and said to the young people, "It's time to get your things."

Senator Morton, their traveling companion and friend of Mrs. Taft, stepped down from the carriage and reached up to assist Mandie's grandmother.

Everyone scrambled for their handbags and followed.

Mandie, firmly holding on to her white kitten, gasped when she finally noticed the huge building they were about to enter. It seemed to go completely out of sight on each side. Even well-traveled Jonathan was surprised—it was absolutely monstrous.

"This doesn't even look like a house!" Mandie said.

"Not like one I've ever seen," Celia added.

"It is rather large, isn't it?" Jonathan agreed. "I can't wait to look around tomorrow morning, when we can really see how big it is."

Mandie stepped ahead to catch up with her grandmother. Tugging on her sleeve to get her attention, Mandie asked, "Grandmother, how many people live here?"

"It's only the Thaler family and their servants, as far as I know, dear," Mrs. Taft told her. "I've known the Thalers for years and have visited with them in other houses they own in Europe, but I understand they bought this one only recently."

Uniformed servants seemed to be hovering everywhere in the dim light from the gas sconces by the doorway. They were taking the bags and directing everyone inside.

The three young people followed the adults into an enormous stone-walled hallway lit by more gaslights. An older woman in a black uniform approached them. She spoke directly to Mrs. Taft. "Madam, welcome, I am Hedgewick, the housekeeper," she said smiling, her gray-haired head bobbing beneath its white cap. "Madam Thaler regrets that the family was suddenly called away to Germany because of the illness of her mother. She offers you her home for as long as you wish."

"Oh, dear," Mrs. Taft said. "I hope her illness is not serious."

"We do not know yet, madam," the housekeeper replied, turning to the servants who were bringing in the luggage. "You will take the madam's things to the green suite and the gentleman's to the blue suite. The young people will stay in the east wing." The uniformed men moved on with the bags, and Mrs. Hedgewick turned back to Mrs. Taft. "Now, if you will be so good as to follow me, I will show all of you to your rooms. This way, please."

The woman led the way up a wide, curving staircase at the end of the front hall. The walls along the steps were covered with ancient portraits and other paintings interspersed with metal armor, swords, and antique guns. There were gaslights everywhere.

Mandie whispered to her friends as they brought up the rear, "This place looks like an armed fortress." Snowball, content in his mistress's arms, settled back to sleep.

"It probably is—used to be, I should say," Jonathan told her. "These walls must be hundreds of years old."

"Hundreds?" Celia stopped in surprise.

"Don't forget, Europe is old," Mandie reminded her. "Even Uncle Ned will be impressed with this place."

"When did Uncle Ned say he would get here?" Celia asked, as they continued up the stairway.

"Probably tomorrow," Mandie said. "He seems to have friends everywhere. He has become aquainted with a lot of important people who move around the world. His work to help the Cherokees has made him well known, too. He had to stay in town to visit someone when we got off the train."

"Town is a long way off," Jonathan said. "We've been traveling in the carriage since way before dark, remember."

A clock struck twelve somewhere within the house. Mandie paused to count. "Twelve o'clock—midnight," she announced.

The housekeeper arrived at the top of the stairs and waited for Mrs. Taft and the Senator.

"I'm sorry I'm so slow. I guess I'm not as young as I used to be," Mrs. Taft said, laughing as the senator took her arm and assisted her to the top step.

"But I am *too* fast," the housekeeper replied with a smile. "I go up and down all day. Down this corridor, please." She led them down a long hallway to the left.

"This must be a mile long!" Mandie whispered to her friends, as they hurried to keep up with the others. She shifted Snowball in her arms.

The housekeeper ushered Mrs. Taft into a suite of rooms while the others waited in the doorway. Inside, a maid was already unpacking valises.

"This is lovely, thank you," Mrs. Taft told the woman.

"Now I will need to know where you are putting the young people. This house is so large I may have trouble finding them."

"Of course, madam," the housekeeper replied, crossing the hallway to open another door. "This is the gentleman's suite."

"Thank you," Senator Morton said, taking a look inside. "I'll go along with you to see where the other rooms are."

Everyone followed the woman down several hallways and through heavy doors that divided the wings of the house. The group fell silent as they took in the surroundings. The place seemed empty.

Finally, the housekeeper stopped and opened a door. "These are your rooms, young ladies," she said, "and young man, you will be across the hall." Mandie noticed how deserted this part of the house was and how far away from the adults they would be.

"Will Uncle Ned have a room in this wing, too?" Mandie asked the woman, as she and Celia stepped into the suite they would share.

"Uncle Ned?" the woman questioned.

Mrs. Taft spoke up. "He's not really her uncle, just a family friend. He will be coming out from town tomorrow. I don't know if I mentioned him to Mrs. Thaler when she invited us to stay here."

"There is plenty of room, madam," Mrs. Hedgewick said. "And if the young people would like him to stay in this wing, I will have the maids prepare another suite first thing in the morning."

"Oh, thank you!" Mandie said. "I really appreciate that." She breathed a sigh of relief. This huge house, with its dark shadows and dim lights, was eerie. And with her grandmother all the way across in the other wing, she felt deserted. Uncle Ned, her father's Cherokee friend, had always looked after Mandie since her father's death. Uncle Ned had promised Jim Shaw to take care of Mandie, and he'd kept his promise. Her friend wasn't here yet but he would arrive.

The housekeeper smiled at Mandie, then crossed the hallway to open the door to Jonathan's suite. A servant was inside unpacking his luggage.

"Amanda, can you and Celia and Jonathan remember the way to my suite in case you need me?" Mrs. Taft asked, as she and the senator turned to follow the housekeeper.

"Yes, ma'am," the three chorused.

"Just knock on my door if y'all need anything, no matter what time of the night," Senator Morton told them.

"Thank you," Mandie said for them all.

"Breakfast is served at seven o'clock, but since you arrived so late, if you'd rather have it later I could arrange it," the housekeeper said to Mrs. Taft.

"No, no, seven o'clock will be fine," Mrs. Taft replied. Turning back to the young people she said, "Be sure you are all up and dressed in time. Good night now, and sleep well."

Mandie rushed to her grandmother and stood on tiptoe to plant a kiss on her cheek. Mrs. Taft embraced her, returning Mandie's sudden show of affection.

"Good night, Grandmother, I love you," Mandie whispered.

"You are my pride and joy, dear," Mrs. Taft said,

gently pushing a wisp of hair under Mandie's bonnet.

Mandie rejoined Celia and Jonathan in the hallway.

"Good night, Mrs. Taft, Senator Morton," Jonathan said.

"Yes, good night to y'all," Celia added.

The three stood there in the dimly lit corridor watching the adults until they disappeared around a corner.

"Well, here we are in Switzerland," Jonathan commented, thrusting his hands into his pockets.

"Yes, here we are, and it all seems so spooky," Celia said, shivering.

"Celia, I'm sure it won't seem that way in the morning when the sun comes up," Mandie said, "especially after Uncle Ned gets here." She untied her bonnet and removed it with one hand, still holding Snowball with the other.

"But remember, Uncle Ned said there was a mystery about this house—or chalet, as they call it here in Switzerland," Jonathan remarked.

"I know, and as soon as he comes we'll see if we can find out what it is!" Mandie exclaimed.

"I guess we'd better say goodnight so we can be up in time for breakfast," Jonathan told the girls as he turned toward his open doorway. "Besides, I need to see where my belongings are being put. See you both in the morning."

He went into his suite as the girls said good night.

As Mandie and Celia entered their rooms, Mandie saw a maid hanging her clothes in a large wardrobe in one of the bedrooms off the large sitting room.

"I suppose this will be my room. Those are my

clothes," Mandie remarked as she and Celia stood watching.

"Yes, miss," the young maid said in perfect English. "And we have supplied a commode for your kitten in the water closet." She showed them through a doorway into an enormous bathroom with gleaming marble surfaces and gold-plated fixtures. She gestured toward a large ceramic flower pot filled with sand at the end of the big bathtub.

"But how did you know about my kitten?" Mandie asked in surprise.

"We did not know until we saw you get out of the carriage with him. Then we sent the houseman to fill this pot and place it here," the maid explained.

"Thank you. I appreciate it, and I'm sure Snowball appreciates it," Mandie said with a little laugh.

The maid turned to Celia and said, "Your bedroom is on the other side of the sitting room, miss." She led the way, then opened the wardrobe to display Celia's neatly arranged clothes. Celia removed the bonnet from her auburn curls and dropped it onto the dresser.

"Thank you. You are very efficient," Celia said.

The dark-haired girl smiled and asked, "Is there anything you young ladies would like before I retire?"

When the girls assured her they had everything they needed, the maid bid them good night and left, closing the door to the hallway behind her.

Mandie put Snowball down and removed his red leash and collar. He shook himself, washed his face, then began exploring his new surroundings.

The two girls inspected everything too. There was an outside door in Celia's room. They checked it and found it locked securely.

"I don't care if it is locked, Mandie. I don't like outside doors in my room," Celia complained. "I won't sleep a wink."

"Oh, Celia, you can sleep with me. These beds are big enough for three people anyway," Mandie said, leading the way back into her bedroom. "Besides, I think it's kinda cold, don't you?"

Celia laughed nervously. "Mandie, you don't have to make up excuses on account of me. I just plain don't like this big dark house."

"I tell you what," Mandie said. "We'll just leave the light burning all night in the sitting room. That way, at least we can see if we get scared."

Celia got her nightclothes, which were laid out in her room, and came back to Mandie's to get ready for bed.

Even though it was after midnight, the girls lay awake talking. Snowball curled up at their feet and went to sleep.

"This year sure has been wonderful," Mandie began. "And the best thing of all is this trip to Europe with my grandmother and the senator, getting to travel on a real ship, meeting so many people, and seeing so many places. Meeting up with Jonathan has been one of the best things."

"Yes, 1901 will be a year I'll always remember," Celia replied.

"You know, I've certainly had some adventures— more than most thirteen-year-old girls," Mandie said, giving Snowball a little shove as he rolled onto her foot.

"I'll say—some adventures," Celia said. "Some of the most scary experiences I've ever heard of, much less lived through. And all the dangerous people we've come in contact with . . ." She scooted up a little on her big pillow. "Mandie, please, let's don't get involved with any more mysteries while we're here in Europe. Let's just enjoy our trip like *normal* girls would."

Mandie gave a little laugh and said, "But, Celia, look at the mysteries we've solved and the people we've been able to help. Besides, I think it's fun using your brain to solve things."

"Well, let's let Uncle Ned use his brain to solve the mystery about this house. He's the one who mentioned it in the first place, and I don't think it's our business," Celia said.

"He'll help us," Mandie said. "But I do wish he had given us a hint of what the mystery is all about."

"Remember he said in Rome that there was a mystery about this house. That's all. Maybe there isn't anything to solve. Maybe it's just someone's notion that there's a mystery," Celia suggested.

"Uncle Ned wouldn't have mentioned it if he didn't know there was something—Snowball, what's wrong with you?" Mandie interrupted herself as her kitten suddenly sat up and gave a little growl. She raised up on one elbow to look at him in the dim light.

Celia instantly sprang up in the bed. "Mandie, he hears something. Look at his fur—it's all ruffled up!" she whispered.

"Celia, I don't hear a thing," Mandie said. She listened for a moment. Suddenly she realized there was another growl coming from outside the sitting-room door.

Celia heard it at the same time. She clutched the bedcovers. "There's something in the hall!" she managed to whisper.

"Right," Mandie agreed, as she quietly slipped out of bed and reached for the poker standing by the open fireplace.

She tiptoed across the room and into the sitting room to the closed hall door. She listened silently for a moment. Celia had followed, but stopped at the doorway to Mandie's bedroom.

Suddenly Snowball jumped down from the bed and rushed to the hall door. Mandie snatched him up and cautiously opened the heavy door a crack to peek outside. She couldn't see anything in the dim hallway. Pushing the door open farther, she said, "There's nothing out here." She closed it, returned the poker to the fireplace, and shook Snowball—who had calmed down by now. "Snowball, you gave us a false alarm!"

"But, Mandie, I heard a growl outside the door," Celia insisted as they got back into the big bed. Snowball settled down again at their feet.

"I thought I did, too. But it must have been Snowball making that noise," Mandie said.

"But why was Snowball so upset then?" Celia asked.

"Maybe he heard a rat or something," Mandie said, poking her pillow into place.

"A rat?" Celia asked, frightened. "Mandie, I hope this house doesn't have rats in it!"

"Snowball won't let them bother us," Mandie replied. "Celia, we'd better go to sleep. Good night."

"You're right," Celia agreed. "Good night."

The girls had finally relaxed and were slowly drifting to sleep, when Snowball jumped up, agitated. Celia and Mandie both heard heavy footsteps in the hallway. They seemed to pause outside the sitting-room door.

Celia began to whisper and Mandie clapped her hand over Celia's mouth and said softly, "Sh-h-h-h!"

Again Mandie slipped soundlessly out of the big bed, grabbed the poker, and crept to the sitting-room door. As she got closer, she saw the doorknob turn. This time she paused in fright. Celia had followed her, and Mandie could tell by the look on her face that Celia had also seen the knob turn.

The girls stood still, waiting to see who would open the door. They held their breath and Mandie grasped the poker more firmly. A few seconds passed and nothing happened. There was no more movement at the door.

Finally Mandie got up courage and said loudly, "I'm going to see who is messing with our door!" She grabbed the knob and flung the door open. No one was there. She and Celia both peered into the dark hallway. It was empty.

Mandie closed the door and leaned against it for a moment as she contemplated the situation. "I know there was someone out there. I distinctly saw the doorknob move!"

"So did I," said Celia as she sat down on the carpet, "and I'm scared. My legs won't hold me up any longer."

"We could just leave the door open for the rest of the night," Mandie said. "Then we could see everything."

"Oh, no, please!" Celia pleaded as she got to her feet. "Isn't there any kind of latch or lock on the door?"

Mandie bent down to examine it. "Of course. Look, there's a bolt." She tried unsuccessfully to move it. Then she jabbed at it with the poker but it still wouldn't move.

"Mandie, you could wake up everyone in the house with all that noise," Celia warned her.

"Everyone in this house?" Mandie looked incredulously at her friend. "You know very well there isn't anyone in this big wing except us and Jonathan. Jonathan! Do you suppose he could be playing tricks on us?"

Celia thought for a moment. "No, I don't think he'd do that, especially not tonight, when we're all so tired from our journey."

"I'm not so sure he wouldn't," Mandie said, as the girls went back to bed. "But let's not mention the noises to anyone. Just in case he had anything to do with it, he'll think he failed to scare us, all right?"

"Whatever you say," Celia said. "I'm going to try to get to sleep."

"Me, too," Mandie replied, as she snuggled down under the bedcovers.

Snowball walked around in circles on top of the girls' feet, then finally settled down to sleep.

Mandie thought of her friend Joe Woodard back home in North Carolina. If only he were here, he could help them figure out what all these things were about.

Joe usually tried to discourage Mandie from getting involved in an adventure, but when he saw she was determined to go ahead, he would join her. And Mandie had not run into a single mystery that they couldn't solve.

She finally drifted off to sleep, and dreamed of Joe and the log cabin at Charley Gap where she and her father had lived until his death. Uncle Ned had helped her find her wealthy kinpeople, but Joe had remained her loyal friend.

She dreamed of Joe's promise to get her father's house back when he grew up and became a lawyer. For this she had promised to marry him.

Now she relived all this in her dream. As she stood looking at her father's log cabin, she could hear strange music that seemed to float down with the breeze from the mountainside. She strained her ears but couldn't understand a word of the song.

Chapter 2 / Was It Singing?

Mandie awoke the next morning with the sunlight streaming in across her face. She rose in her bed to see where she was, then remembered. She was in the Thalers' chalet in Switzerland. Celia Hamilton, by her side, was already awake and stretching lazily. Snowball was roaming around the suite.

"No one has called us. What time is it?" Mandie asked, anxiously jumping out of bed to look at the huge grandfather clock in the sitting room. "It's only six-thirty, but the sun is so bright I thought it was later." She went back to flop down on the big bed.

"I was so worried last night, that it took some time before I finally went to sleep," Celia remarked, sitting up beside her friend. "But I kept waking up every now and then. Sometime during the night I heard singing— imagine, someone singing in the middle of the night!"

Mandie quickly looked at her. "Singing? I dreamed

I was back at Charley Gap and heard singing coming from the mountain. It wasn't very clear. I couldn't make out the words."

"Neither could I," Celia said, pushing back her auburn curls. "But it was a woman's high soprano voice."

"That's what I heard, too," Mandie said quickly. "How could we both hear the same thing? I thought I dreamed it, but you actually heard it?"

"I'm sure I did. I was wide awake," Celia insisted. "I thought it would take forever to get back to sleep. The singing had already stopped before I dozed off again."

"Hmmm!" Mandie mused thoughtfully, as she got up to walk around the room. "Do you suppose I was really awake and heard the same singing you did? I don't know, though. My dream was so clear. I could see our log cabin at Charley Gap, and there was Joe Woodard standing under the chestnut trees."

"Maybe you were really dreaming, but you actually heard the same singing I did," Celia said, reaching for her clothes.

"I guess that's possible," Mandie agreed. "I was so tired after that long journey, I was in a daze when we went to bed. Oh, well, I guess we'd better get dressed for breakfast." She went to the wardrobe to choose a dress for the day.

Celia took the clothes she had worn the day before and went to her bedroom to find a fresh dress.

Mandie had dressed and was standing in front of the gilt-edged mirror in the sitting room, trying to pin up her long, blonde hair, when someone knocked at the door. Half-turning, she called out, "Come in!"

She watched in the mirror for the door behind her

to open, but nothing happened. After waiting a couple of seconds, she dropped the hairpins on the table and went to open the door.

"I said, come in!" Mandie quickly opened the door and looked out into the long wide hallway. There was no one there. "Well!" she sighed. She started to close the door, but at that moment Jonathan came out of his suite across the corridor.

"Good morning!" he called.

"Good morning, Jonathan. Did you just now knock on our door?" Mandie asked.

"As a matter of fact, I did. But I had forgotten my handkerchief, so I ran back to get it," Jonathan explained with a impish grin.

"Well, at least that's accounted for," Mandie said, turning back into the room. "I suppose you can come in and sit here by the door, provided we leave it open. But you'll have to watch Snowball; he might go out into the hall. We'll be ready in a minute, and then we can go sniffing for food."

"Thanks," Jonathan said, sitting down in a small chair by the open door. He picked up Snowball, who was rubbing against his ankles.

Mandie picked up the hairpins and went into Celia's bedroom. Celia was already dressed and tying a ribbon in her hair.

"Are you not going to put your hair up?" Mandie asked.

"I don't have time. It takes me so long. What about yours? Let me brush it and tie it back for you," Celia offered.

"Thanks, Celia. I don't think I'll ever learn how to put

my hair up right," Mandie complained as she sat down.

Celia quickly brushed out Mandie's long hair, took a ribbon from her bureau, and tied back the blonde tresses. She inspected it and decided, "There. I think it looks nice that way."

Mandie stood up to look in the mirror and said, "It's an awful lot of hair to hang so loose, but I suppose it'll have to do for right now. Jonathan is waiting for us to go to breakfast." After Mandie put Snowball in his red harness and fastened his leash, the three young people hurried down the long, deserted hallway.

At the first heavy door dividing the hallway, they couldn't agree which way they had come the night before. The corridor went in three different directions.

Jonathan told them, "I'm sure we came straight down the hallway. We shouldn't make any turns now."

"Well, I suppose if we go the wrong way we can always turn around and come back and go another way," Mandie decided, as they followed Jonathan's directions.

They soon came to another dividing door across the hallway. "Let's just keep going straight ahead," Jonathan suggested.

As they went through the doorway, they met a maid in a trim uniform hurrying toward them from the other end of the corridor.

"I am sorry for the delay in coming to wake you for breakfast," she apologized as she came up to them. Mandie noticed an accent in her speech. "We just found out that the maid for your wing is ill this morning. We hadn't realized until now that you had not been called for the morning meal. So if you will please follow me."

"That's all right," Mandie said, as they followed the girl. "I hope the other girl is not seriously ill."

"She's not a girl, miss. She is an elderly lady and she has bad days now and then," the girl explained. "Anyway, I will be your maid while you are here. My name is Helga."

"Thank you, Helga," Mandie replied, as they went on. "My name is Amanda, but I'd rather be called Mandie, and this is my friend Celia Hamilton, and my friend Jonathan Guyer."

Helga turned to look at Jonathan as they came to the wide staircase leading down. "Jonathan Guyer? Your father is Mr. Jonathan Lindall Guyer, am I correct?" she asked.

"Why, yes, he is, but how did you know?" Jonathan asked, puzzled.

"Your father, he is well-known here in Europe. I read about your disappearance in the newspapers," Helga told him while they walked down the steps.

"Please, let's not talk about that," Jonathan said. "I am now in the care of Mrs. Taft and Senator Morton, until my father comes for me, or until my relatives in Paris return home so I can stay with them."

After going through several hallways and doors, Helga finally stopped before a heavy, ornate door. She opened it, and they saw Mrs. Taft and Senator Morton seated at a small, white-covered table.

"I will feed kitty." Helga offered, reaching for Snowball's leash.

"Oh, thank you," Mandie said, handing over the red strap as Snowball looked up and meowed at his mistress. Mandie stooped to tell to him, "This lady is going to feed you while we eat. You be good now." Rising, she said to Helga, "After he eats would you please bring him back to me? I'm not sure what we'll be doing today and I don't want to lose him in this great big house."

"Yes, certainly," Helga answered, pulling lightly on the leash. "Come along, kitty." She walked off down the hallway with Snowball trying to race ahead of her.

When everyone had exchanged greetings, they all sat down and Senator Morton returned thanks for the meal.

"Sorry we're late, Grandmother," Mandie said.

"I understand, dear. I heard that the housekeeper didn't know y'all hadn't been called until a few minutes ago," Mrs. Taft said. "Now that we are all here, let's help ourselves to this wonderful food. The custom here for breakfast seems to be that the servants put the food on the table and leave us to wait on ourselves."

"Just like home," Mandie said, with a sigh. "Will it be all right if we go looking around afterward, since the owners are not home?"

"I think so, dear," Mrs. Taft replied. "The housekeeper told us to make ourselves at home."

Senator Morton sliced a piece of ham and said, "I understand the original part of this chalet is well over two hundred years old. That would be the center section where we entered last night. Now the house has dozens of rooms."

Mrs. Taft added, "Besides the acres and acres of gardens, and several cottages among the trees at the back. There is also a lake." She sipped her coffee, then said, "Y'all be careful around the water though."

Mandie had other things on her mind. "I'd like to

know when Uncle Ned is going to get here," she said.

Celia looked at her and immediately nodded.

"Amanda," Grandmother said, "what in this world are you going to do when Uncle Ned can't keep up with you? He is getting pretty old, you know."

Mandie laid down her fork and sighed. "I don't know. I realize Uncle Ned can't live forever, but I just don't know what I'll do when he's gone."

"Cheer up," said Jonathan with a smile. "He may live to be a hundred, and you'll be all grown up and won't need him by then."

But Mandie didn't smile back. "I'll always need Uncle Ned. He helps me through all my trials and troubles," she said solemnly, clasping her hands together.

Senator Morton changed the subject. "I'd like to see the lake. How about if I come along with you?" he asked, looking around the table.

Mrs. Taft quickly added, "There is a stable of horses, and a small cart and driver to carry us around the estate."

"Horses!" Mandie and Celia said together.

"Yes, *real* horses," Jonathan teased.

"My mother raises horses on our farm in Virginia, you know," Celia said to Jonathan.

"And my father always kept some horses when he was—when we lived at Charley Gap," Mandie said. She turned to her grandmother and exclaimed, "Let's go see the horses when we finish eating!"

Mrs. Taft consented and even agreed to go along with them.

After Helga, the maid, returned with Snowball, they all walked out to the stable. There were several purebred horses, which were friendly with the girls. They stuck their big noses through the fence for Mandie and Celia to pet them.

The dark-haired stable boy, Eckart, hitched a pony to a small cart and everyone piled in for a tour of the estate.

As they drove out of the thick trees surrounding the house and stable, huge snow-covered mountains came into view in the distance. The young people gasped in wonder.

"Is that really snow up there on those mountains?" Mandie asked, squinting to shield her eyes from the sun as she sat on the seat behind the stable boy.

"Yes, miss, it really is," Eckart told her as he stopped the cart for them to look. "Those are the Alps."

Several snow-covered peaks rose into the clouds, but the valley between Mandie and the mountains seemed to be covered with brightly colored flowers.

Celia said breathlessly, "It's almost unreal to be warm and sunny down here, and to look up there and see snow on the mountains."

"This is an amazing country," Mrs. Taft remarked. "I wanted you girls to see the Alps. Jonathan has probably seen them during his school days here."

"How far away from them are we?" Mandie wanted to know.

"A long, long way, over rough terrain," Eckart explained. "The mountains look close because they are so big and so high."

They continued on in the cart and soon came to the lake. The smooth, clear water was surrounded by flower gardens in full bloom. The girls giggled with delight as

Eckart pulled up near the glimmering pool.

Snowball tried to wriggle free of Mandie's grasp, so she suggested they all get out of the cart and walk around. Mandie noticed a small stone cottage standing in a clump of trees near the flower gardens.

"Does someone live in that house?" she asked the driver.

"No, miss," he replied. "Mr. Thaler has not yet decided what he will do with it. You see, they've only been here a short time, and they have not taken care of everything yet. There are several cottages near here that are completely furnished. Servants live in two of them, but this one is not occupied."

"Who lived here before the Thalers?" Mandie asked.

"Oh, miss, the former residents are all dead. The family lived here for many generations. Mr. Thaler was kind enough to employ some of them because they had been born here and had no place to go," the boy explained. "Would you like to see the courtyard behind the chalet?"

"Of course," Mrs. Taft said. "Are we too far away to walk?"

"No, madam. We are close. I'll show you the way," Eckart said, walking along the narrow road, leading the horse and cart.

They passed through a stand of trees and found themselves suddenly at the back of the chalet. Before them lay a courtyard paved with uneven stones, terraced into several levels descending to an inlet from the lake. Fountains spouted among hundreds of flowers and shrubs. Two great stone lions on pedestals guarded the rear entrance.

"Everything is so green, so fresh, and so beautiful!" Mandie exclaimed.

"And it all smells so good!" Celia added.

Mrs. Taft and Senator Morton wandered off among the flowers and sat on a stone bench near one of the fountains.

The young people looked up at the grand chalet. From the rear they could see it was three stories high. There was a tower and a room at the top with curtained windows, and a small balcony projected from it over the courtyard.

"That's interesting!" Jonathan remarked.

"Is that tower room anywhere near our rooms?" Mandie asked, holding tightly to Snowball's leash.

"I do not know which are your rooms, miss," the boy said.

"We are staying in what the housekeeper called the east wing," Mandie explained.

"Then you are on that side," Eckart pointed to his left. "This is the north side of the chalet. The front faces south."

Celia asked, "Does anyone use the tower room?"

"No, miss, that part of the house has not been renovated yet," Eckart said.

"Could we go up there and see it?" Mandie asked.

Eckart cleared his throat and hesitated. "Why, I don't really know, miss. You see, none of the servants go up there."

"Why don't they?" asked Jonathan. "Aren't they responsible for taking care of the whole place?"

"Yes, they will look after the entire chalet once renovation is complete, but right now I think it would be impossible to get anyone to show you that tower," Eckart said, dropping his gaze.

Mandie sensed a mystery at once. "Is there something wrong with the tower?"

"We don't—really know, miss," the boy responded with some hesitation. "You see, the villagers claim the tower is—haunted."

"Haunted?" Mandie exclaimed. Her blue eyes sparkled with the thrill of discovery.

"Please, we must not get into details," Eckart quickly replied. "The Thalers won't appreciate my talking to you about it."

"But why?" Mandie asked.

"Miss, I really think I should return to the stable if you do not need my services," said Eckart, turning to the bush where he had tethered the pony. "If you wish the cart again, please let me know."

The boy jumped into the cart and drove back through the trees.

Jonathan, Celia and Mandie looked at each other, and then up at the tower.

"Do you think the tower is really haunted?" Celia exclaimed.

"There's no such thing as a place being haunted," Mandie declared. "There's some kind of mystery about it, and I imagine that's what Uncle Ned was hinting at."

"And you plan to solve it, right?" asked Jonathan.

"Right," Mandie affirmed.

Celia warned, "Mandie, we might get in trouble. Eckart said the servants don't go up there, so how are we going to get up there? Besides, it looks awfully spooky."

"Spooky? How can it look spooky from way down

here on the ground?" Mandie asked.

"But it *sounds* awfully spooky," Celia corrected herself. "I don't think we should go poking around up there."

"I have an idea this must have been the front of the chalet in its early days," Jonathan speculated. "You can tell the wings have been added to the rest—there is a slight difference in the color of the stone. And all the old places I have seen in Europe have the tower right in the front, if there is a tower. And Senator Morton did say this center section is the original house."

"I suppose we'll have to walk all the way around to the front door to get back inside," Mandie remarked.

Mrs. Taft and the senator started walking down the path around the chalet and called to Mandie. She and Celia and Jonathan followed the adults and examined the chalet as they walked by. The additions had lots of windows, but the original structure had hardly any. They also noticed a side door in the east wing.

As Mrs. Taft and the senator arrived at the front door, Mrs. Taft asked Mandie if they were going to come in.

Mandie looked at her friends. "I suppose so," she said. "I'd like to see the inside of the house."

Jonathan and Celia agreed.

Mrs. Taft cautioned them, "Just remember to conduct yourselves in a fitting manner, and don't do anything rude." Turning to the senator, she said, "Let's ask the housekeeper where the sitting room is."

The senator followed Mrs. Taft down the hall, and Mandie turned to her friends, "Let's go upstairs." She picked up Snowball and hurried toward the staircase at the far end of the corridor with Jonathan right at her heels.

"Where are we going, Mandie?" Celia wanted to know as she rushed to keep up with the other two.

"I don't know exactly. We can just explore."

Jonathan agreed. "Let's look around the original part of the house."

When they arrived at the top of the stairs, it looked familiar.

"We've been through here before," Celia noted aloud.

"You're right," Mandie said, holding Snowball more firmly.

"There should be a corridor going to the back," Jonathan puzzled.

"That's right, because the tower is at the back of the house," Mandie added.

Celia shivered when she heard this.

"I don't see any way to get through to the back of the house," Mandie said. She opened the doors along the hallway. "These are all bedrooms and sitting rooms."

"There has to be a way back," insisted Jonathan as he looked into the rooms.

Mandie thought for a moment and said, "Probably a secret door or something, right?" She went into a room and examined the walls.

Jonathan did the same while Celia watched.

"Nothing in this room," he declared.

"Mandie, are you looking for a secret door like the one in your Uncle John's house—the one that leads into the secret tunnel?" Celia asked. "Here, let me take Snowball."

Mandie handed him to her friend and said, "I suppose it has to be something like that." She and Jonathan continued searching the room.

They worked their way all the way down the corridor to the east wing, then back to the west wing without finding any passage to the back of the house.

Finally they sat down in one of the sitting rooms to discuss the situation. Celia set Snowball down and allowed him to walk while she held his leash.

"There has to be a way," Mandie insisted.

"Unless there really is a deep, dark secret that has caused them to seal up the tower," Jonathan suggested.

"That's it!" Mandie agreed.

Helga appeared in the doorway with instructions from Mrs. Taft. She asked that they go downstairs to the parlor immediately.

"Oh, shucks," Mandie sighed, as the others rose to follow the maid. "We would have to leave now, when we had just figured out what the problem must be." She picked up Snowball and followed the others.

"We can come back if you want to," Jonathan told her.

"Let's do, as soon as we get a chance," Mandie said.

She wondered why her grandmother had sent such an urgent message. It wasn't time for tea. What could she want?

Chapter 3 / Strangers Arrive

Mandie's thoughts stopped immediately when Helga showed them into a parlor where the adults were waiting. There sat dear Uncle Ned in his deerskin jacket! He was all smiles as Mandie thrust Snowball into Celia's arms and ran across the room to embrace her Cherokee friend.

"Oh, Uncle Ned, I'm so *glad* to see you! You just can't imagine how glad I am to see you!" Mandie cried excitedly as he put an arm around her, and pulled her down onto the settee next to him.

"Papoose all wound up?" Uncle Ned puzzled, smoothing Mandie's long blonde hair. "See papoose just yesterday! What excitement about?"

Mandie caught a brief glimpse of Helga standing in the hallway outside the room. She looked at her grandmother, and then the senator. She gave Jonathan and Celia a knowing look as she replied, "I can't tell you right

37

now, Uncle Ned. We can talk about it later."

Her remark made Mrs. Taft stare curiously at Mandie, so she quickly resumed speaking before her grandmother could ask any questions, "Uncle Ned, you should see the outside of this house! And the grounds and the gardens—and everything. And, oh yes, the beautiful horses. You'd love the horses!"

Uncle Ned smiled broadly. "I see these horses, Papoose. I ride horse from town. I leave him at stable."

"You rode a horse all the way from town? You must be tired!" Mandie said.

She jumped up suddenly and stopped Helga in the hallway. "The housekeeper said she would have a room prepared for Uncle Ned in the east wing. Do you know if the room is ready?"

Helga smiled at her. "Indeed it is, miss. Does the gentleman wish to go to his room now?"

Everyone overheard the conversation, and Uncle Ned rose to join Mandie and Helga in the hallway. "Yes, I clean up now."

"I'll go with you, Uncle Ned," Mandie said. "I just want to see where your room is."

"Amanda!" Mrs. Taft spoke sharply. "Let Uncle Ned have some time to himself. You can wait for him here."

Mandie stopped in the doorway and pleaded, "But, Grandmother, I only want to see where his room is. I'll come right back. I promise."

"I'll go with her, Mrs. Taft," Celia volunteered, handing Snowball to Jonathan.

"I sense something afoot here, Amanda," Mrs. Taft said. "If you are planning another one of your escapades in this house, you'd better forget it right now. You and

Celia return here immediately after you see where Uncle Ned's room is. No secret planning!"

"Of course not, Grandmother. And thank you," Mandie said, as she and Celia followed Uncle Ned and Helga.

Mandie didn't want Helga to hear any of her conversation with Uncle Ned, so they spoke very little. Helga led them to a suite next to the girls'.

"You'll be right next door to us!" Mandie exclaimed.

"Does the gentleman wish anything else?" Helga asked Uncle Ned.

"No. Thank you," he replied as they all stepped inside the luxurious suite.

"The bathroom facilities are right through this door," Helga explained, crossing the sitting room to open a door on the far side. The bathroom was modern and up-to-date for 1901. "If you need anything else, I am at your service."

Helga bowed slightly and left the room. Mandie watched through the open door as Helga went on down the hallway. Then she grabbed Uncle Ned's hand.

"Uncle Ned," she said, "things have been happening around here!" Mandie described the events of the night before while Celia listened.

"Today we found out about the tower that the stable boy says is believed to be haunted," Mandie continued. "Was that what you were talking about when you said there was a mystery about this house?"

Uncle Ned smiled and sat down on the settee. The girls joined him. "Papoose, these all tales," Uncle Ned replied. "Must be answer to haunted tale and noises Papoose hear. We find answer."

"I knew you would help us, Uncle Ned," Mandie said

gratefully. "We have not told Jonathan about last night, because we weren't sure if it was he who was trying to scare us. Do you think we should tell him?"

"Yes. Yes. With all haste tell Jonathan boy," Uncle Ned answered. "Look at face. See if he guilty. I think not so."

"We will, Uncle Ned," Mandie said, standing up to leave. "We have to go now. Do you think you can find your way back through all these hallways and doors? We could wait for you."

"No, no. Papoose promise grandmother come back. Go now. I find the way," he said, waving the girls out of the room.

"Thank you, Uncle Ned. I'm so glad you're going to be next door to us," Mandie called back to him as she and Celia hurried into the hallway.

"Mandie, what are we going to do about this mystery?" Celia asked as they walked along.

"We need to talk to Jonathan, like Uncle Ned said, and then we need to discuss all this in detail with Uncle Ned. He can help us, I know," Mandie told her.

"Don't forget what your grandmother said about becoming involved in an adventure in this house," Celia reminded her.

"Oh, I know, but we aren't going to become involved in anything. We're just going to figure out what's going on," Mandie assured her.

"But if we're going to figure out what is going on, then won't we be involved in whatever it is?" Celia wondered.

"We won't do anything wrong, I promise you," Mandie said.

"Someone might hear us if we go into the hallway at night to check on strange noises," Celia said. "And if we find a way to get into the tower, won't someone see us?"

"Don't worry about it, Celia. I'm sure Jonathan will help us. And we'll just have to be real careful not to get involved," Mandie said.

As they neared the bottom of the stairway to the first floor, they saw the housekeeper talking to a man and a woman at the front door.

"The Thalers are not in residence at the moment," the housekeeper said as she stood with the door partly open. "I am sorry, but you will have to return when they are here."

"But, madam, Mrs. Thaler invited us to be her guests whenever we happened to be in the area," the man said quickly.

"We were planning a visit several months from now, but our plans didn't work out, and we were not able to let them know we would be coming early," the woman added.

"I am sorry, but Mrs. Thaler left no orders for me and I am not in the habit of admitting complete strangers without her permission," the housekeeper insisted. "Now, if you will please come back when she returns."

"When will that be?" the man asked.

"They have been called away on an emergency. I do not know when they will be home," the housekeeper replied. She started to close the door.

Mandie and Celia stood quietly on the bottom step listening and watching.

"Please wait," the man said, sticking his foot out to

keep the door from closing. He set down his luggage, and pulled a folded paper from his pocket. Handing it to the housekeeper, he said, "You see, here is the note we received from Mrs. Thaler. Please read it."

The housekeeper scanned the note and immediately relented. "Why did you not show me this in the first place?" Mrs. Hedgewick asked. "You may come in."

The housekeeper showed the couple to a long bench, and asked them to wait while the maid prepared rooms for them.

Mandie and Celia quickly went on their way before anyone caught them eavesdropping.

"I wonder who they are?" Mandie asked as they walked toward the parlor. She stopped suddenly. "Do you think they'll be put in the wing with us?"

"Let's be real slow, and watch and see," Celia whispered.

"That would take too long. Mrs. Hedgewick has to find the maid to prepare the rooms, and then she has to come back down for the people. And Grandmother will be wondering where we are!"

"You're right," Celia agreed. "We can't wait any longer."

As soon as they entered the parlor, Mrs. Taft said, "Amanda, I think you'd better take Snowball out for a stroll. I don't see a sandbox anywhere."

Jonathan was holding on to Snowball's leash, but the kitten was walking in circles and softly growling.

Mandie hurried to snatch him up. "I'll be back in a few minutes," she said.

"Me too," Celia added, following Mandie into the hallway.

They passed the strangers sitting on the bench, and quickly made their way outside, leaving the front door open.

Mandie let Snowball down in the yard immediately, and looped the leash around a hitching post. She and Celia sat down on the stone steps where they could keep an eye on the strangers inside.

Suddenly Jonathan joined them on the steps. "I thought I'd see what you were up to," he said. "Who are those people inside?"

"We don't know," Mandie whispered, glancing to see if the couple was looking at them.

In a low voice Mandie told Jonathan what they had overheard.

"Are they Americans?" Jonathan wondered.

Mandie and Celia both shook their heads. "I don't think so," Mandie said. "They speak English, but they have an odd accent." She noticed Helga speaking to the couple, who rose from the bench. "Helga is taking them upstairs."

The three watched as the guests struggled with their luggage. It was almost more than they could carry. Mandie quickly unhooked Snowball's leash from the hitching post and picked him up.

"Let's see where they're going," she told her friends.

Mandie led the way with Celia and Jonathan close behind her. They waited until the strangers reached the top of the stairs, and then quickly followed. They arrived at the upstairs hallway in time to see Helga lead the couple in the direction of their rooms.

"They're going to be put in our wing!" Mandie whispered. The three managed to follow out of sight.

Arriving at the prepared suite, Helga opened the door next to Jonathan's and showed the strangers inside. The young people looked at each other and turned back down the hall the way they'd come.

"So they're going to be next door to you, Jonathan," Mandie said when they were far enough down the hall not to be heard.

"That's all right," Jonathan said. "Maybe I'll find out who they are and why they insist on visiting the Thalers' when they aren't at home."

"That is really strange," Mandie said.

"But we're here without the Thalers, too," Celia said.

"That's different," Mandie said. "We didn't know until we got here that the Thalers weren't home—even though they were expecting us."

When they came to the top of the staircase, they paused for a moment.

"I suppose we'll at least find out their names when we go to the dining room for the noon meal," Jonathan said, looking at the big grandfather clock on the landing, "and that's not long from now."

When the young people returned to the parlor, Uncle Ned was there too. Mrs. Taft was saying, "I thought this place here in the country would give us all a chance to relax after all the sightseeing we've done since we got to Europe."

Mandie and her friends took seats nearby, and Mrs. Taft immediately asked, "Did you see the new guests? I wonder who they are?"

"We don't know, Grandmother," Mandie said, explaining how the strangers had been greeted by the housekeeper and then finally admitted to the house.

"I wonder if I might have met them at sometime or other," Mrs. Taft said.

"Did you see them, Mrs. Taft?" Jonathan asked.

"No, no, I didn't. Uncle Ned told us about them. He just happened to be coming back to the parlor and overheard the maid telling them to follow her to their rooms," Mrs. Taft replied.

"And do you know where their rooms are?" Mandie asked. "Helga put them right next door to Jonathan!"

"I understand the adult guests are usually put in the west wing where the senator and I are situated, and the youngsters like y'all are put in the east wing," Mrs. Taft said. "And that's where they put Uncle Ned because you requested it."

"Therefore the housekeeper didn't think they were very important, right?" Mandie added, pushing Snowball off her foot, where he had decided to curl up and go to sleep.

"Evidently," Senator Morton agreed.

"I would imagine they'll be back down shortly and we'll get to meet them," Mrs. Taft said.

The housekeeper appeared in the doorway and spoke to Mrs. Taft, "The meal is on the table, madam. If you will please follow me . . ."

Mrs. Hedgewick showed them into a large dining room where two uniformed maids stood ready to serve from a sideboard. The long table was set with snow-white linen, expensive-looking china, sparkling silver, and shining crystal. Sunshine streamed in through floor-length windows, which were draped in deep green velvet. A huge painting of the Alps hung at one end of the room. Mandie spotted a painting of the Eiffel Tower nearby. She recognized it from her stay in Paris. There were other scenes from various countries in Europe.

As Mandie gazed around the huge room, Mrs. Hedgewick spotted Snowball at the end of his leash. "The animal! Take him to the kitchen! Quickly!" the housekeeper ordered one of the maids.

Mandie gasped, ready to defend her beloved kitten, when Mrs. Taft said, "Amanda, give the leash to the maid."

"Yes, Grandmother," Mandie said, handing the red leash to the younger of the maids. "Please bring him back when we've finished eating. I won't know where to find him."

"Of course, miss," said the girl, smiling as she took Snowball. "I'll see that he gets fed and back to you. Don't worry."

Mrs. Hedgewick was showing them to their places when Mandie noticed there were no place settings for the two strangers. She could tell her grandmother was also mentally counting the place settings.

"Are the other guests not dining with us?" Mrs. Taft asked.

"No, madam. They preferred to have something in their rooms, so they could rest," the housekeeper explained. "They will be down tonight."

The young maid who had taken Snowball to the kitchen returned without the kitten. Mrs. Taft assured Mrs. Hedgewick that everything was fine, so the housekeeper left the room.

The maids hovered around the table, serving the food and filling cups, so that Mandie and her friends were hesitant to say much to each other during the meal. Even Mrs. Taft seemed unusually quiet, and Senator Morton, who never had much to say, was silent. Uncle Ned, still in his deerskin jacket, quietly observed everything.

Mandie, unable to determine what some of the food was, ate only familiar foods and hot rolls, and Celia only nibbled at certain things. Mandie noticed Jonathan partook of everything that was offered to him.

Uncle Ned spoke to Mandie across the table, "We eat, then we talk, Papoose."

Mandie quickly smiled at him and said, "Oh, yes, Uncle Ned. As soon as we are finished eating we can talk."

Mrs. Taft, overhearing them, said, "I thought we could all go for a walk after this wonderful meal. Unless you have something important to discuss with Amanda, Uncle Ned."

"No. We talk later. Walk first," Uncle Ned agreed. He smiled and sipped his coffee.

Mandie sighed in disappointment. She knew her Indian friend must have something important to talk about, or he wouldn't have made a point of mentioning it to her. But they wouldn't have a chance to talk privately with her grandmother around. She'd just have to wait.

Mrs. Taft glanced around the table. "If everyone is finished, shall we go outside?"

Everyone got up, and Mandie asked the maid for Snowball.

"I will have him here in a whisk," the girl told her as she left the room.

Mandie felt her ribbon slip from her hair as she stood. As she reached for it, her hair loosened.

"Grandmother, I need to re-pin my hair," Mandie said, as the maid came back with Snowball and Mandie took his leash.

"Go ahead, dear, we'll be right outside the front door, waiting," Mrs. Taft told her, as she and Senator Morton started to leave the room.

"I'll go with her," Celia said, following Mandie through the doorway.

"I think I'll run up to my room a minute, too," Jonathan added.

Mrs. Taft looked at the young people and shook her head. "Now be sure you all get back down in a few minutes. We will be waiting." Turning to Uncle Ned, she said, "Come on, Uncle Ned, let's get some fresh air."

Taking no time to talk along the way, Mandie, Celia and Jonathan hurried toward their rooms. Nearing Jonathan's door, they found the door to the strangers' suite partly open. They slowed their steps as they approached the door and heard talking inside the room.

"Well, at least we got inside the house," the man was saying.

"Yes, but it may not do us any good because of the other guests," said the woman.

The three young people stopped in their tracks.

The man continued, "I don't think that makes any difference. They are Americans, after all."

Snowball lurched unexpectedly, jerking the leash out of Mandie's hand. She went after him.

"Snowball, come back here!" she called.

Jonathan and Celia followed, hearing the strangers' door close as they passed it. Snowball got to the end of the hall and stopped.

Jonathan opened the door to his suite. "I'll be out in a minute. I'll wait for you girls here in the hall."

"All right," Mandie said as she and Celia entered their suite. Mandie went to the mirror, picked up her comb, and began working on her hair.

"What do you think they were talking about, Celia?" Mandie asked.

"Us, I guess," Celia said.

"I know that," Mandie said, pushing a hairpin into her hair. "But it sounded to me like they were up to something."

"Yes, it did," Celia agreed. "Let's hurry and discuss it with Jonathan."

"Yes, let's do," Mandie said, shoving the last hairpin into her thick, blonde hair.

Jonathan was waiting for them in the hallway, and the three hurried back toward the stairs. Mandie held tightly to Snowball's leash.

"If Snowball hadn't run away, we'd probably have heard more," Mandie said.

"We'll just have to keep our eyes and ears open," Jonathan said.

"We sure will. I believe those people are up to something, and I'm going to find out what it is," Mandie said.

"Maybe," Jonathan teased.

Mandie tossed her head and led the way down the stairs.

Chapter 4 / The Room at the Top

Halfway down the stairs Mandie stopped suddenly, causing Celia and Jonathan to bump into her.

"I'm sorry," she said in a low voice. "Jonathan, we need to talk to you."

"About what?" Jonathan asked.

"I'll explain later. My grandmother will be wondering where we are," Mandie said, rushing on down the stairs with Snowball in her arms.

When they got outside, Mrs. Taft, Senator Morton and Uncle Ned were admiring the house from where they stood near the driveway.

"It's such an interesting structure," Mrs. Taft was saying as Mandie approached her. She turned. "Don't y'all agree?"

"Yes, ma'am, it is," Mandie replied. She set Snowball down and held on to his leash. "I think it's awfully interesting," she added, giving a knowing smile to her friends. *If Grandmother just knew how interesting the three of us really think it is!*

Senator Morton and Mrs. Taft led the way down a crooked path, and Mandie tugged at Uncle Ned's sleeve to get his attention as they followed.

Mandie whispered. "We need to talk!"

"Soon," the old Indian said, smiling down at her.

"Real soon, please, Uncle Ned," Mandie said in a low voice.

"Yes," Uncle Ned promised.

After the group had followed the pathway a distance from the chalet, the ground became rough and steep and Mrs. Taft stopped ahead of them.

"I think we'd better turn around and go back," she said. "There's a down-slope ahead."

The others caught up with her to take a look. Mandie thought it looked awfully steep, but she wanted to get away from everyone and talk with Uncle Ned. She purposely released Snowball's leash.

"Amanda! Snowball is loose!" Mrs. Taft said, turning suddenly to her granddaughter as the white kitten raced past her long skirts and on down the steep trail.

"Snowball!" Mandie called, as she watched him scamper away.

"Amanda, you'd better go get him," Mrs. Taft sighed. "I must find a place to sit and rest. Please be careful!"

"I don't believe there's a place to sit until we go back up the pathway," Senator Morton told her.

"Uncle Ned, would you please help Amanda catch her cat? I'm afraid she might fall on that steep bank," Mrs. Taft told him.

"I go." Uncle Ned nodded, and hurried after Mandie.

Jonathan and Celia followed too, while Mrs. Taft and Senator Morton walked back the way they had come.

Snowball scampered down the pathway, stopping now and then to look back at his mistress. Finally his leash, trailing loose from the harness, caught on a bush and brought him to a sudden halt near a retaining wall.

"Aha! I caught you," Mandie said, rushing forward to pick him up.

"Sit," Uncle Ned said to the young people as he gestured toward the low wall. "We talk."

As soon as they sat down, everyone started to talk at once. Uncle Ned raised his hand. "Wait!" Turning to Mandie, he asked, "Did Papoose tell Jonathan boy about last night?"

"No, Uncle Ned. I'm sorry, but I forgot all about it," Mandie replied, as she hooked Snowball's leash onto a bush.

"Tell me what?" Jonathan quickly asked.

"About last night," Mandie said, and with Celia's help she told him about the noises they had heard. She watched his face, as Uncle Ned had suggested earlier. Jonathan seemed truly surprised.

"Why didn't you knock on my door or call me or something?" the boy asked.

"Because we were afraid to go out into the hallway," Mandie said.

"Well, if anything like this happens again, just open your door and yell loud as you can. I think I'd be able to hear you," Jonathan told the girls. "But I think this needs looking into. Have you told anyone else about it?"

"No, we don't know any of the servants really," Mandie replied. "And if I told my grandmother, it would only upset her, or she wouldn't believe us."

"But it really did happen! Both of us heard the noises and saw the doorknob move," Celia added.

"I stay next door, Papoose. I wait. I watch," Uncle Ned promised. "I find who make noise." He stood up to go.

"Wait, Uncle Ned," Mandie said, motioning for him to sit down again. "We have more to tell you."

"Must hurry," the Indian said, sitting down.

The three related what they had overheard from the new guests.

"I think they're up to something," Mandie said.

Uncle Ned listened thoughtfully, then said, "May be right. But Papoose leave this to me. I find out what going on."

"We won't tell anyone else, Uncle Ned, but we're going to be watching and listening," Mandie said. "Now that we've told you everything we know, tell us what the mystery is about this place. What were you talking about when you told us in Italy that there was a mystery about this house?"

Uncle Ned cleared his throat and looked from one to the other as the three waited.

"Old tales," he began. "Villagers say young papoose die with broken heart. Not allowed to marry true love. Her mother and father think love is not good. Some say papoose jumped from window of tower, kill herself. They hear her singing still—at night."

As Uncle Ned related the story, the three young people sat with open mouths and wide eyes. Then everyone tried to speak at once.

"I heard singing last night!" Celia said.

"So did I, but I thought I was dreaming," Mandie said.

"Well, I heard the singing too, but I figured it was one of the servants off on a lark," Jonathan said.

"The tower!" Mandie exclaimed. "Uncle Ned, Eckart, the stable boy, told us the tower was haunted, but then he wouldn't talk about it. And we've tried to find out how to get into it, but there just doesn't seem to be any way."

Uncle Ned looked at Mandie and said sternly, "Papoose must not snoop around strange house. Private business."

"But if we could solve the mystery then the village people would stop telling tales about the house!" Mandie said.

"I'd think the owners would be grateful for a solution to the problem," Jonathan added.

"And the servants wouldn't be afraid anymore," Celia said.

Uncle Ned got up and warned them, "Must not do dangerous things. Grandmother not like either, Papoose. We go now."

Mandie took Snowball's leash from the bush and picked him up. "We'll just keep our eyes and ears open," Mandie said, as they started back up the steep path.

"Papoose must behave," Uncle Ned admonished her. "And you, and you too," he said, turning to Celia and Jonathan.

As they passed a huge tree along the path, Mandie caught a glimpse of a man who seemed to be watching them. Evidently seeing her look at him, he quickly ran off into the woods.

"A man was watching us," Mandie gasped, pointing toward the tree.

"I know," Celia and Jonathan both said.

"Man work here," Uncle Ned said simply.

"He works here?" Mandie asked.

"Plant flowers," the Indian added, taking Mandie's hand to help her over a rocky place in the path.

Jonathan and Celia were holding hands to keep from slipping on the rough terrain.

"I wonder why he was watching us and how long he'd been standing there. Maybe he heard what we were talking about," Mandie said.

Finally they came within sight of Mrs. Taft and Senator Morton, who had found a bench beside a flower bed.

"How did you know who he was, Uncle Ned?" Celia asked.

"See him plant flowers when we go down path," Uncle Ned replied.

"We didn't even notice him," Mandie said. "You see everything, Uncle Ned."

"Not everything, Papoose," Uncle Ned said, smiling.

When they reached Mrs. Taft and the senator, they all started back toward the chalet. As they approached the front door, Mrs. Taft said, "It must be getting near teatime, and I'd like to meet the other guests. Let's look for the maid."

Everyone agreed and they went inside. "I'm anxious to get a closer look at the strangers," Jonathan remarked.

"And I'm anxious to find out how to get into the tower," Mandie said softly.

"Remember what Uncle Ned said," Celia reminded her.

"I will," Mandie assured her.

The housekeeper was in the front hallway and she hurried toward Mrs. Taft. "Would madam like tea now?"

"Oh, yes, please," Mrs. Taft said.

Mrs. Hedgewick led the way to the parlor, and left them to order tea. Mandie closed the huge double doors in order to allow Snowball to roam.

As they waited for tea they all discussed their tours through Europe so far. They had docked in London and had traveled to Paris and Rome. From Switzerland they would go to visit a baroness who had invited them to her castle in Germany.

"Oh, Grandmother, I am having such a wonderful time!" Mandie exclaimed, but then grew solemn as she added, "But I do wonder what my mother and Uncle John are doing while I'm gone."

Mrs. Taft was sitting on a dark red velvet sofa with Senator Morton. "I'm sure your mother is fine, dear. Your Uncle John has taken good care of her since their marriage, and I know they're both happy."

"Yes, and with the new baby they probably don't even miss me," Mandie said, straightening her long skirt and looking down at her feet. Celia, sitting by her side, drew in a deep breath. She knew it was a touchy subject—that new baby.

"Amanda, you shouldn't say things like that," Mrs. Taft reprimanded her. "When will you realize that your mother and your Uncle John don't love you one iota less since that baby came?

"I know. I'm sorry, Grandmother. I guess I just miss

my mother," Mandie said, and then she quickly added, "But I can't have everything; I had to leave my mother to come on this journey. I'll really try to love the baby when I get back home."

"You won't have much time at home, you know," Mrs. Taft reminded her. "You and Celia will have to go back to school just a few days after we get home."

"My mother said I'd only have time to get packed at home in Richmond, then return to school in Asheville," Celia said.

"I don't even know what I'll be doing," Jonathan said, "whether my father will come and take me home, or whether I'll stay with my aunt and uncle when they get back to Paris. You girls should be thankful you know what you will do." He looked a little sad as he stood up to gaze out the huge window nearby.

At that moment the housekeeper opened the door and ushered in the maid with the tea cart. Mandie tried to see what was on the trays.

Mrs. Taft asked, "Will the new guests be in for tea?"

Mrs. Hedgewick frowned. "They are still resting it seems—taking tea in their rooms. Surely they will be down for the evening meal."

"I was just wondering if I might know them," Mrs. Taft said. "Are they Americans?"

The maid placed a tray on the small table in front of her. "No, madam," Mrs. Hedgewick replied. "They come from France. Their name is Bagatelle."

"Bagatelle," Mrs. Taft repeated. "No, I don't believe I know anyone by that name."

"I do not know them either, madam," Mrs. Hedgewick said. "I have never seen them before nor heard the

Thalers mention their name." She inspected the trays and asked, "Is everything satisfactory, madam?"

"Yes, it is, thank you," Mrs. Taft replied.

"Then we will leave you to enjoy your tea," the housekeeper said, motioning to the maid to leave the room with her.

Mrs. Taft leaned forward to pour the tea. The young people readily accepted the sweet cakes. They hadn't realized how hungry they were after their long walk. Mandie gave Snowball some crumbs on the hearth.

"My curiosity is stirred," Mrs. Taft said, passing out the cups of tea. "I wonder just who these people are. You'd think the housekeeper would have at least heard of them."

Senator Morton took a sip of the hot tea and said, "If they ever decide to be sociable and come down to eat, maybe we'll find out more about them."

"Maybe your aunt and uncle know them," Mandie suggested to Jonathan between bites of the delicious cake. "They come from France."

Jonathan laughed and said, "France is a big country, Mandie. Remember?"

"But your kinpeople are newspaper people. And newspaper people know almost everybody, don't they?" Mandie said.

Jonathan smiled at her and said, "Not quite. But if it will give you any satisfaction, I'll ask them if they know my relatives—that is, if we ever get to meet these strangers."

Senator Morton changed the subject. "I understand there is an observation room at the top of the chalet. Would you youngsters like to help me find it?"

The three friends beamed and responded, "Oh, yes, please!"

Mandie caught a warning glance from Uncle Ned, and she knew what he was thinking. They weren't to go poking into anything that didn't concern them.

"Are you coming with us, Uncle Ned?" Mandie asked.

He smiled at her and nodded. "I go with Papoose."

"And I will be resting in my suite while you people traipse around," Mrs. Taft announced.

Everyone rose and Mandie scooped Snowball into her arms.

They asked directions from the housekeeper, who told them the observation room was at the top of the west wing. They had to pass Mrs. Taft's and Senator Morton's suites to get there, so Mandie's grandmother went with them as far as the door to her suite.

"We are headed toward the back of the house," Mandie remarked as they walked down the hallway. "Uncle Ned, do you think this observation room connects with the tower?"

"No, Papoose," the Indian said, holding a heavy door open that divided the corridor. "This room is to left, tower is to right."

"Yes, that's right," Mandie agreed. "We're headed for the corner, and the tower is in the center of the original part of the house.

"I wonder why they have an observation room and a tower," Celia asked. "Don't they both serve the same purpose—observing the grounds around the chalet?"

Senator Morton answered her as they opened another door and discovered a set of steep steps. "You're right. However, I understand the tower is in unstable condition and needs a lot of work done on it before it can be used. The room we're headed for is much newer."

The three young people stole quick glances at each other. Mandie thought Senator Morton might be right about why the tower was closed off, but it certainly didn't look unstable from the outside. *We have to find a way to explore it,* Mandie thought.

Senator Morton led the way up the steep, narrow staircase. Mandie carried her white kitten.

At the top, they emerged into a large room with floor-length windows on two sides. The windows were all open, and fresh clean air filled the room. There was an assortment of antique furniture, including a couch placed in front of the windows, where one could sit and view the landscape. Chairs, and tables with ornate candlesticks completed the furnishings. A multicolored carpet covered most of the stone floor. The walls were of smooth, gray stone.

The young people quickly surveyed the room and walked to the floor-length windows at the back side of the house. A small balcony extended out from the window, without any railing. A gable of the roof met the bottom of the balcony.

Celia quickly stepped back. "It's too high for me, and nothing to hold on to if you should fall!"

"Oh, yes. Please be careful," Senator Morton cautioned them as he and Uncle Ned joined them at the window briefly, then walked to the other side.

Mandie let Snowball down and held firmly to his leash, while she and Jonathan quietly discussed the room.

"These are thick stone walls. I don't see any way to get in and out of here except by the stairs," Mandie said.

Jonathan leaned forward to look over the balcony. "Unless you could climb from this balcony onto the roof. You might come up somewhere near the windows of the tower."

Mandie followed his gaze, trying to see what he saw without leaning over the balcony. "Maybe, but it sure would be scary. One slip and you'd fall a long way."

"You'd have to use ropes, like mountain climbers use. That way, if you slipped you'd have something to hang on to," Jonathan said.

"I'd rather find another way to get into the tower," Mandie said. "Besides, where would we get the ropes?"

"I saw some rope in the stables," Jonathan replied, as he stepped away from the window and collided with Celia. "Sorry."

"Y'all are not really going to climb out on that roof, are you?" she asked.

Mandie tried to sound nonchalant. "We might, if we can't find another way to get into the tower. But you don't have to go with us, Celia, if you're afraid."

Celia moved closer between her friends and looked out. "It looks awfully steep."

"Look! There's that gardener watching us again," Mandie said excitedly, pointing to a man behind a large tree below. The man, half hidden by the trunk, was definitely looking in their direction.

As the three crowded closer to get a glimpse, the man disappeared into the woods.

"I wonder why he watches us?" Mandie mused.

"Maybe we'll get a chance to ask him why," Jonathan said.

"Maybe he never see Indian before." Uncle Ned was suddenly behind them.

The three turned in surprise. They hadn't heard Uncle Ned approach.

"That's probably why he's always staring," Mandie agreed.

"I don't like the idea of his watching us," Jonathan said.

Neither do I, Mandie thought. *The gardener might catch us out on the roof heading for the tower! How can we stop him from spying on us?*

Chapter 5 / Looking for an Entrance

After their visit to the observation room, Celia suggested they go to the stables to find out if there were horses they could ride. Uncle Ned agreed to go with them, but Senator Morton said he would rest until it was time for the evening meal. Mandie took Snowball with her.

Eckart was cleaning the stables while the horses were all outside. When he saw the four guests approaching, he stopped sweeping.

Mandie spoke for her friends. "Eckart, are there some horses we could ride?" Snowball strained on his leash to explore the stable.

"I'm afraid not, miss," Eckart replied, glancing at Uncle Ned. "You see, the horses are not ridden much here, and they would be difficult to handle."

Jonathan spoke up, "But we've all ridden enough to know how to handle a horse."

"What shall we do, Uncle Ned?" Mandie asked. "Where is the horse you rode from town?"

"Outside." Uncle Ned pointed to the paddock. "We must walk."

"But what about the cart?" Mandie asked. "Eckart, could we please have the cart and pony, please? We won't be gone long. Uncle Ned can drive us around the property."

Eckart looked curiously at Uncle Ned, then asked, "Is he your uncle?"

Mandie laughed and said, "No, not really. He's my dearest friend, and since he is lots older than I am, I call him Uncle Ned. In fact, everyone calls him Uncle Ned."

"But," Celia told the stable boy, "Mandie is really part Cherokee Indian, like Uncle Ned's people."

"You are an Indian?" Eckart asked Mandie with surprise.

"My grandmother was Cherokee. That makes me one-fourth Indian," Mandie explained proudly.

"I see," Eckart said.

Jonathan spoke up, "Well, are you going to let us use the cart?"

"Oh, yes, of course," Eckart quickly responded. "I'll get it ready."

Mandie and her friends waited while Eckart got the pony from the paddock and harnessed him to the cart.

Uncle Ned stepped up and took the reins as Celia and Jonathan hopped onto the back seat. Mandie, holding firmly to Snowball, sat up front with Uncle Ned.

"Well, where are we going?" Celia asked.

"Just for a ride around the property," Mandie replied.

She turned to Eckart. "How will we recognize the borders of the Thaler estate?"

"That will be easy. There's a split-rail fence all the way around the Thalers' holdings," Eckart explained. "But let me warn you; the property is quite large. Don't get lost! He pointed to a trail that led off behind the stables. "That trail goes completely around the property."

"Thanks," Mandie replied. "With Uncle Ned along we won't get lost. We'll be back soon."

Everyone waved to Eckart as Uncle Ned drove the cart down the trail.

They rode through trees and shrubs and came into an open meadow filled with brilliantly colored flowers in full bloom. In the distance they could see the snow-covered Alps. Nearby was a branch of the lake they had visited earlier.

The scenery was so overwhelming to Mandie that she excitedly asked Uncle Ned, "Can we please stop and walk through those beautiful flowers and smell the blossoms? They are *so* gorgeous!"

Uncle Ned smiled and drew the cart to a halt. The young people jumped down as he tethered the pony to a fencepost. Mandie handed Snowball's leash to Uncle Ned, and raised her long skirts to wade through the thickly growing blooms, stopping here and there to bend and smell the fragrance. Celia and Jonathan followed. Uncle Ned walked Snowball around the cart and waited for them.

"Did you ever see such flowers?" Mandie excitedly asked her friends.

"Not this many at one time," Celia said.

"Not solid fields of them like this," Jonathan added.

As the three bent over to inspect a flower they had never seen before, a sudden angry voice brought them upright.

"Stop!" the male voice boomed nearby. "Do not touch!"

The young people spun around to see the gardener staring at them. Mandie recognized him as the one who had watched them from below when they were in the observation room, but he looked much older now. He was a tall man, and his chubby face was distorted with anger.

"We were just looking," Mandie explained.

"Do not walk among the flowers!" the man said. "Get back on the trail!"

Uncle Ned walked over to them to see what was going on. The man saw him approach and was visibly shaken.

"An Indian!" the gardener gasped, backing away from them. "Go! Now!"

"Come, Papoose," Uncle Ned told Mandie. "We go now."

Mandie looked at Uncle Ned, then turned to the gardener. "Why do you spy on us? We see you everywhere."

"I am not a spy. I am the guard of the chalet," the man replied, and quickly disappeared into the trees.

Everyone climbed back into the cart.

"So he is a *guard*," Mandie said, taking Snowball into her lap.

"He must have thought we were going to pick the flowers," Celia fussed.

"He was angry," Jonathan commented, "but he was also intimidated by Uncle Ned."

Uncle Ned straightened his deerskin jacket and said, "Man not like Indian." He picked up the reins and they were on their way again.

"I'm sorry, Uncle Ned. Maybe they don't have Indians here in Switzerland. I don't think they dislike you. You're just different to them," Mandie said.

"Big God made Indian," Uncle Ned said, reaching to clasp Mandie's hand in his old wrinkled one. "Always, Papoose, be proud what Big God made."

Mandie tightened her hand in his, smiled up at him and said, "I am, Uncle Ned. I'm proud God made me part Indian. I'm proud of all my Cherokee kinpeople. I just wish people wouldn't act so funny around Indians."

"I don't act strange around Indians," Jonathan announced.

"Neither do I, Mandie," Celia added.

Uncle Ned quickly swung the cart around in a wide place in the trail and headed back the way they had come. He laughed and said, "Now we find way back."

Everyone laughed.

"That's easy," Jonathan said. "We just go back the way we came."

"But Uncle Ned knows how to find his way anywhere," Mandie said proudly. "He taught me how to mark bushes along a trail, and how to tell direction by the sun and the way the creeks flow, and so many other things."

As they rode back toward the chalet, Jonathan leaned forward and asked Uncle Ned, "Tell me, do you think there could possibly be some secret way out of the observation room into the tower?"

"Maybe," the Indian said. "But I not see a way from room but by steps we used."

"Let's go around the house and look at the observation room from the outside," Mandie suggested as Uncle Ned turned the cart into the stable yard.

Eckart came out to take the pony and cart. After thanking him, the young people and Uncle Ned walked around to the back of the chalet to look up at the observation room and the tower. Snowball tried to race ahead on his leash.

They found they were too close to see anything that high up. Uncle Ned led them down the slope to look back up.

Mandie pointed. "There's the observation room and there's the tower. They don't join each other, but there does seem to be some kind of attic or something between them. Look!"

Everyone nodded. There was a rise in the roof between the room and the tower. The rest of the house seemed lower.

"Are we going up inside that room again?" Celia asked.

"Could we, Uncle Ned?" Mandie eagerly asked.

The Indian hesitated for a moment. "We look. We not poke in house of others."

The young people quickly led the way back through the front door and up the stairs.

"Remember," Mandie reminded her friends as they reached the top of the stairs, "we don't go toward the wing we're staying in. We have to go back in the section where Grandmother and Senator Morton have their suites."

"Quiet," Uncle Ned warned as they rushed forward.

Mandie led the way and the others silently followed down the long corridors and through the heavy doors. When they arrived at the door to the observation room stairs, they stopped.

"Now which way?" Mandie asked. Snowball squirmed on her shoulder.

"To right," Uncle Ned said. "Look for more steps. Must go up."

The young people moved along the corridor, opening doors and carefully examining rooms along the way. They found only lavishly furnished bedrooms and sitting rooms. Another heavy door divided the hallway, and as soon as they passed through it, they realized they were in the servants' quarters. The rooms appeared occupied and were meagerly furnished. The corridor dead-ended into a solid wall.

"Oh, shucks!" Mandie exclaimed.

"No way to get up there," Uncle Ned said, looking around. "We go now. Time to eat." They all turned to go back the way they had come.

"Wait!" Mandie said, stopping everyone. "Let's just look out the window from one of the rooms here and see exactly where we are." She quietly opened a door nearby and looked into the room. It appeared to be a sitting room.

"Careful," Uncle Ned cautioned. "Papoose not disturb room of others."

Jonathan and Celia followed Mandie as she softly slipped across the room and pulled back the curtain. They gazed outside, bending this way and that, trying to get a better look.

"Come," Uncle Ned said quietly from the doorway. "We go."

They obeyed him, and Mandie closed the door to the room. As they started back down the hallway, Mandie let Snowball down on his leash.

"I couldn't tell exactly, but don't y'all think we were right beside the wall of the tower?" Mandie asked.

"Since the wall is flat there, I couldn't tell for sure either, but I believe you're right," Jonathan agreed.

"Outside can tell," said Uncle Ned, smiling.

"I don't know how we could tell from the outside. All I could see from the room were a lot of trees and shrubbery," Mandie said, holding tightly to Snowball's leash while he strained to run ahead.

"Papoose go outside, look," Uncle Ned said.

"All right, let's go outside and see if we can tell where we were," Mandie agreed.

"Must hurry. Soon time to eat," the Indian reminded them.

They rushed back downstairs, out the front door, and around to the back of the chalet. Uncle Ned led the way down the slope far enough so they could see the high walls of the house above them. He stood there waiting, observing them while they looked.

"Let's see, it must have been that window," Celia said, pointing to a small window near the location of the observation room.

Jonathan disagreed. "No, it was nearer the middle of the house."

Mandie stared at the windows, puzzled by Uncle Ned's confidence, until her gaze traveled along the wall and stopped at the room where they had just been.

"There, there, there!" she exclaimed, pointing. "We didn't push the curtain back in place! We *were* right next to the tower!" She turned to smile at Uncle Ned.

"It's the last window before the tower wall on that end of the house," Jonathan confirmed.

"Well, we only found a blank wall," Celia said. "I don't see why you're both so excited."

"You're right, Celia," Mandie said, calming down. She looked at her friend and said, "It was a blank wall, and there's no way to go through it."

Jonathan suddenly gasped. "There's someone in that room! It looks like one of the strangers."

Mandie quickly looked up. She could see a man standing in the room, too. He looked out and then dropped the curtain into place. "You're right, Jonathan, it was that man!"

"Yes," Uncle Ned said, unimpressed. "Now we eat."

"You sure must be hungry," Mandie teased. She laughed and picked up Snowball.

"We not be late for meal," the Indian replied. "We visit here."

"Of course, Uncle Ned," Mandie agreed. "We must have good manners while we are guests in someone's house."

When they entered the front hall, Helga was coming down the stairs.

"I went to announce to you that dinner is ready to be served, but you were not there," the maid told them.

"Is my grandmother in the dining room yet?" Mandie asked.

"Madam is waiting in the parlor," Helga said, reaching for Snowball. "I will take the kitten to the kitchen to eat."

"Thanks, Helga. Please bring him back when he's finished," Mandie said, as she followed her friends to the parlor.

Mrs. Taft and Senator Morton rose as soon as the others entered the parlor.

"The meal is waiting," Mrs. Taft said to Uncle Ned.

"Yes, maid tell us now," he replied.

"We went for a ride in the cart, Grandmother," Mandie began as the housekeeper came to the doorway to take them to the dining room. "And then we explored part of the house."

"Yes, dear," Mrs. Taft said absentmindedly to Mandie, and then turned to speak to Senator Morton as they walked down the hallway. "Surely the other guests will be at the table tonight. I didn't want to ask the housekeeper again if they would be."

"If they have any manners at all, they will be present," Senator Morton replied.

Mandie overheard the conversation and whispered to Jonathan, "That man is probably still upstairs in that room."

"Right," Jonathan said.

"Are we going to tell your grandmother we saw him there?" Celia asked, softly.

"Maybe," Mandie said, stepping ahead to take Uncle Ned's hand. "I want to sit by you, Uncle Ned."

The old Indian pulled out a chair for her and then sat down in the next seat. Jonathan sat next to Celia across the table from them. Mrs. Taft and the senator were near the end of the table. Mandie noticed her grandmother looking for extra place settings again. Evidently the strangers didn't want to be sociable. *I wonder why?* Mandie thought. *And what was that man doing in the servant's room?*

Senator Morton returned thanks and as soon as they settled down to eat, Mrs. Taft spoke. "Uncle Ned, I have some friends coming to visit tonight," Mrs. Taft said. "They live a few miles from here. They'd like to meet you."

Uncle Ned smiled and said, "Your friend my friend."

Mrs. Taft smiled back at him and turned to the young people, "Now if y'all don't want to sit through the visit, you may find something else to do. I only caution you to remember that we are guests here and you should act accordingly."

"We'll find something to do, Grandmother," Mandie quickly replied.

"Yes, ma'am, I'm sure we will," Celia said.

"Yes, ma'am," Jonathan echoed.

Uncle Ned frowned at Mandie.

He knows we'll try to explore the house for a way into the tower, and he won't be there to help us, Mandie thought.

As soon as the meal was over, Mandie, Celia and Jonathan sat on the steps in the front hall. The maid brought Snowball back and tied his leash to the bannister.

"Well, looks like this is our chance to explore!" Jonathan said, grinning at the girls.

"Yes," Mandie agreed, "but we need to plan this thing out instead of running around all over the place without accomplishing anything."

"Mandie," Celia said, standing to shake the wrinkles out of her long skirt, "I'd like to go to my room and freshen up first."

"That's a good idea," Mandie said, unhooking Snowball's leash from the bannister.

"I'll meet you girls in the hallway outside our rooms in about ten minutes," Jonathan told them. They all jumped up and ran up the stairs to get ready.

As they rushed down the corridor in their wing of the house, Mandie suddenly slowed. "Let's be quiet when we pass the strangers' suite," she whispered. "We might hear something."

"Right," agreed Jonathan.

But as they walked by the strangers' door, they found it closed. Nothing could be heard from the hallway.

"Hurry!" Jonathan told the girls as they all went into their suites.

Inside the sitting room, Mandie put Snowball down and took off his collar and leash. "Snowball, I'm going to take a chance and leave you in my room," Mandie told the kitten as he frolicked across the floor, happy to be free. "You're a lot of work to carry around all the time."

"Why don't we put a note on the door saying, *Watch out for the cat,*" Celia suggested.

"That's a good idea!" Mandie said, going for some writing paper on the desk. While Celia went into her bedroom, Mandie wrote the note, *Beware of the cat,* and held it up for Snowball to see.

"You can guard our rooms while we're gone, Snowball," she said to the kitten, who meowed and rubbed around her ankles.

As the girls left the suite, Mandie stuck the edge of the paper into the door frame so that it was held securely when the door was shut. Celia laughed at what Mandie had written and so did Jonathan when he saw it.

"Some watchdog that cat would make!" he laughed.

"You don't know Snowball," Mandie said. "He is smarter than people give him credit for."

"Let's go sit in the parlor at the top of the stairs and discuss our strategy," Jonathan suggested.

"Yes, let's do," Mandie agreed.

At that moment the door to the strangers' suite opened and the man looked out into the hallway. When he saw the three, he turned to the woman who was behind him and said, "Not right now." Then he shut the door.

"Well!" Mandie said. "Let's hurry to the parlor. If they leave their rooms and go into the other wing they'll have to pass the parlor door."

As they hurried down the corridor, Mandie wondered why the strangers didn't want to speak to them. *They act as though they are trying to hide from everyone,* she thought. *Well, we'll catch up with them sooner or later.*

Chapter 6 / What Are the Strangers Up To?

Mandie, Celia and Jonathan sat in the parlor with the door almost closed. They only talked in whispers while they listened for any footsteps approaching. The room was situated across from the hallway landing of the main staircase and toward the west wing of the chalet. If anyone went into the west wing, they'd have to pass the parlor, as far as the three young people could figure out.

"We could sit here all night and those people may never come this way," Mandie whispered to Celia and Jonathan, beside her on a settee in the room.

"I have an idea it's going to take a lot of waiting and patience to solve the mystery surrounding those strangers and the mystery of the tower," Jonathan said softly.

"And I have an idea they are connected," Celia whispered.

Mandie quickly asked her, "You mean you think the strangers have something to do with the tower?"

"Yes, I do," Celia replied. "Why would that man be in the servant's room after we were in there? In fact, what was he doing in the servants' quarters anyway?"

"That has me puzzled too," Jonathan said.

"Well, yes, it does look like he followed us there. Maybe he thought we were searching for the entrance to the tower," Mandie whispered.

"But why would he be interested in the tower?" Jonathan asked. But he quickly answered his own question, "Because they've heard the tale of its being haunted. According to Eckart, everyone around here has heard the story."

"Of course," Mandie agreed. "And they're trying to find a way into the tower, just like we are."

"Oh, goodness," Celia exclaimed. "I hope we don't get tangled up with those people."

"But the housekeeper said they were from France," Mandie said quietly. "Do you think they'd come all the way from France just to investigate a haunted tower? Besides, the housekeeper said they had a note written to them by Mrs. Thaler inviting them to stay here. But even though Mrs. Hedgewick says they are French, they were speaking English when we overheard them in their suite."

"Maybe they knew the Thalers before the Thalers bought this chalet, and as soon as the Thalers moved in, Mr. and Mrs. Bagatelle found out about the tower and decided to come and visit," Jonathan said.

"Anyway," Celia said, "if we overhear them speaking in French, Jonathan can always translate for us."

Mandie quickly stood up, shaking the folds out of her long skirt, and said, "I'm tired of waiting. Let's go look around the servants' quarters."

The others agreed, and Mandie pulled the door open and stepped into the hallway. She almost bumped into the Bagatelles, who were headed for the west wing.

The woman spoke rapidly in French to Mandie as she and her husband stopped. Jonathan and Celia joined Mandie.

Mandie shook her head and said, "I'm sorry, but we don't understand French. We're Americans."

The woman, a tall brunette who looked like she could adorn the cover of some fashion magazine, smiled at Mandie and spoke in English, "I am sorry. I only said 'excuse me for running into you.' Goodbye." She and her husband, also tall, dark-haired, and handsome, continued on their way into the west wing without even looking back.

"Well, that was abrupt," Mandie declared as she watched the couple disappear down the corridor. "Let's give them time to get ahead and then we can follow them without being seen."

"What for, Mandie?" Celia asked.

"Oh, Celia!" Mandie exclaimed. "That's what we've been sitting here waiting for, to see if they go into the servant's room we were in this afternoon. If you'd rather stay here and wait for us, it'll be all right."

"No, no, I am going with you," Celia replied.

"All right. Let's go. Remember to be very cautious and quiet," Jonathan told the girls. The three headed in the same direction the couple had gone.

They finally spied the couple walking ahead of

them—down the long corridor that led into the servants'
quarters. Jonathan motioned for the girls to step inside
an open doorway with him where they could watch and
see where the Bagatelles went. Slowly and silently, the
three moved along a few doorways at a time until the
strangers boldly opened the door to the servant's sitting
room where the young people had been earlier. The
couple entered and shut the door.

As the young people hovered in a nearby doorway,
Mandie exclaimed, "How are we going to know what
they're up to in that room?"

"Maybe there's a keyhole," Jonathan whispered.

"Come on," Mandie whispered, leading the way to
the big heavy door to the room.

Celia and Jonathan followed and they quickly examined the door for a keyhole. There was a big keyhole,
but there was evidently a key in it on the other side,
filling up most of the space in the hole.

Mandie leaned over and put her eye to the hole. "I
can't see anything," she whispered. "The key is in the
way."

Jonathan tried it and agreed.

"I have an idea," Mandie suggested. "Let's get a key
from another room and poke the key out by sticking
the other key in from this side." She hurried around to
examine nearby doors. After three doors, she found a
key.

She rushed back to the closed door and slowly
poked the key into the keyhole. For a moment, the key
on the other side of the door did not budge. But then
it turned in the lock and fell out on the other side, thud-
ing on the hard floor. The young people gasped and ran
for hiding.

Evidently the strangers ignored the key and didn't come out, so Mandie once again peeked through the keyhole. This time she could see. The man and woman stood looking out the window. Mandie moved away and motioned for Jonathan to look and then Celia. The three looked at each other, silently puzzled about what was going on inside.

Mandie signaled for the others to follow her to the room where she had borrowed the key. She pushed the door almost shut and slipped the key into the keyhole.

"I don't understand what they're doing, just standing there, do y'all?" she whispered.

"No, not unless they are watching for someone or something below in the yard," Jonathan said.

"Or they could just be standing there figuring out what they plan to do next," Celia said.

Suddenly there were footsteps in the hallway. The three young people peeped out just as Helga stepped into a room nearby.

"Thank goodness this isn't Helga's room," Mandie said, looking about. "In fact I don't believe anyone stays here. I don't see any personal belongings."

The others agreed.

They heard the couple open the door to the sitting room.

"I thought I locked this door," the man said.

"But the key is on the floor. Maybe it just fell out," the woman said.

"I'll just take this key with me," declared Mr. Bagatelle. "That way no one can lock this door so we can't get in."

"We may not need to get inside again," Mrs. Bagatelle replied.

The youngsters carefully withdrew into the room where they were hiding as the couple walked past and on down the corridor toward the main staircase.

When they were out of sight, Mandie said, "Now, Helga is in her room right down there, so we'll have to be careful and not let her hear us."

The others silently nodded their heads as Mandie led the way to the room the Bagatelles had just left. She pushed open the door and they went inside. The curtain was pushed back completely away from the window. The group looked around but found nothing different from their previous visit. It just looked like a normal sitting room.

Mandie pushed open a door leading to an adjoining room and found a bedroom, furnished but evidently unoccupied.

"Look! I don't believe anyone lives in these rooms," Mandie said softly.

The others looked around and agreed. The three walked back to the window to look outside. At that moment, the hall door opened and they spun around, fearing they had been caught where they should not have been. It was Helga, who seemed as startled at finding them in the room as they were at being discovered.

Before the maid could speak, Mandie quickly said, "We were admiring the grounds from up here. It's such a beautiful place."

Helga looked at them suspiciously and said, "Yes, it is. But, miss, this is the servants' quarters. I do not believe the housekeeper would like it if she found you here."

"We're sorry," Jonathan quickly told her, and the

three started toward the door, leaving the curtain pushed back.

"We really are sorry," Mandie added. "You see, while my grandmother has visitors tonight, we were told we could look around the house."

"Yes, miss, that's fine," Helga said. "But I really think you should stay out of this part of the house. The servants wouldn't like it if they found you snooping in their rooms." She stood inside the room watching them.

"We truly are sorry if we've offended you. We'll leave right away," Celia said as the three went into the hallway.

Helga stood in the doorway and watched them until they went through the heavy dividing door down the corridor. The young people kept looking back to see what she was doing.

Once they were out of Helga's view, they stopped to talk.

"What do you suppose Helga was doing in that room?" Jonathan asked.

"I don't know, unless she was checking to see if it was clean and done up right," Mandie said. "But, you know, she might just have a secret too. Remember, Jonathan, she knew who you were as soon as we got here, and who your father is."

"Oh, Mandie, everyone here can't have a secret," Celia said.

Jonathan smiled and said, "You never know."

"Let's go see if the Bagatelles went back to their suite," Mandie suggested, and she led the way back toward their wing.

When they came to the Bagatelles' suite, they found the doors closed, and even when they stood close by and listened they couldn't hear a thing.

"If they're in there they aren't talking," Mandie whispered.

"Why don't we go back up to the observation room and look it over again?" Celia asked.

"That's a good idea," Mandie agreed.

"It's getting dark outside and we probably won't be able to see much outdoors from up there," Jonathan told the girls, and then with a mischievous tone he added, "But we could explore the whole room inch by inch."

"I don't know what we'd be looking for, because we found out that it isn't connected to the tower," Mandie said, but they started back the way they had come anyway. "I guess we could decide if we want to go out on that roof to get over to the window of the tower."

Celia shivered and said, "Not me. I'll just watch out for y'all if y'all decide to do that."

When they arrived at the observation room, they were surprised to find the Bagatelles sitting on the settee. The Bagatelles were also surprised to see them. The young people hesitated in the doorway and after saying "hello" to the couple, they walked across the room to the windows on the front of the chalet.

The Bagatelles returned the greeting and carried on a conversation in rapid French. Jonathan looked over his shoulder at them now and then, but they didn't seem to notice.

"I wonder if that gardener is down there somewhere," Mandie said, as the three gazed down onto the dusky grounds.

"Probably," Jonathan said, turning his head slightly

to listen to the French couple.

"I can't see anything. It's already too dark and all the trees make it even darker," Celia remarked.

The Bagatelles soon stood up and left the room, still carrying on a rapid conversation in French. Jonathan stepped softly to the doorway to be sure they were gone. He took a look down the stairway to see if they were out of earshot.

"What were they saying, Jonathan?" Mandie quickly asked.

Jonathan smiled and said, "They think none of us understands French because of what you said to them before. But I got an earful. The woman was saying, 'We don't have to worry about these young people because they can't understand a word we're saying if we speak in French.' Then the man said he thought *it* could be done."

"What could be done?" Mandie asked.

"He didn't say, he just said, 'Yes, I think it can be done.' And then the woman said, 'If we take our time, I don't believe anyone will realize what we're doing.' That's about all they said," Jonathan reported.

"They are definitely up to something," Mandie decided. "We'll have to watch those people. They might have figured out how to get into the tower."

"But we don't know for sure that they are trying to get into the tower," Jonathan reminded her.

"Everything sure sounds like it," Celia spoke up.

"And if it's not the tower they're talking about, then they're up to something else that they don't want anyone to know about," Mandie said.

"We'll just have to beat them into the tower," Jonathan said, turning to look out the windows again.

Mandie asked him, "You aren't thinking about going out on that roof tonight, are you?"

"It would be better if we could do it at night. That way we would be less likely to be seen, and if the moon is out, we'd have plenty of light to find our way over to the tower," Jonathan said.

"But we don't even have any ropes," Mandie reminded him.

"That's right. We can't do it tonight, but tomorrow I'll borrow some rope from the stables, bring it up here, and hide it while you girls attract Eckart's attention somewhere else," Jonathan told them. "We can take the rope back later."

"I don't think I want to go out on that roof," Celia said.

"You don't have to, Celia," Mandie said, and with a sudden flash of inspiration she added, "You can watch for us from down in the yard and signal if anyone shows up."

"All right, I'll do that," Celia agreed.

Jonathan bent over to look outside and said, "We can anchor the rope around this beam between the windows here, and after we get outside we can loop it around that chimney over there." He pointed out the window along the roof. "And from there we can swing over to that window you can see there in the tower."

"I suppose you've given up on trying to find an entrance to the tower somewhere around that room in the servants' quarters," Mandie said, straightening up to look at him.

"There just isn't an entrance there," Jonathan said.

"We won't be able to get out on the roof here until tomorrow night, so we could keep looking around that room tomorrow if you girls want to."

"Let's keep looking for a safer way, at least," Mandie replied.

But they went ahead with their plans for the next night just in case they didn't find an entrance in the servants' quarters. In the middle of their planning, Uncle Ned appeared at the doorway of the observation room to tell them Mrs. Taft had sent him in search of them.

"Uncle Ned," Mandie said, "have Grandmother's visitors gone home?"

"Gone," the old Indian assured her. "Papoose come now to parlor."

They followed him back to the parlor where Mrs. Taft and the senator waited to bid them good night.

"It's late, dears," Mrs. Taft said, rising to return to her suite. "I just want to say 'sleep well' now. We'll be up early in the morning."

They all went up the staircase to their various rooms. Back in their suite, Mandie and Celia got ready for bed. Snowball was so excited about seeing Mandie after being shut up so long that he cut capers around the room.

As she slipped into the big bed with Celia, Mandie said, "I hope Grandmother doesn't have plans to take up our whole day tomorrow. We need some time to explore those rooms. We might find some way that wouldn't be as dangerous as climbing out on the roof."

Celia plumped up her pillow and said, "Are you afraid to go out on the roof, Mandie?"

"Well, not really," Mandie said, hesitatingly. "But I'd like to find another way."

"Are we going to tell Uncle Ned so he can help us?" Celia asked.

"Oh, no, no," Mandie quickly turned over to look at her friend. "We can't tell him. He might tell my grandmother, and she'd probably put a stop to it all."

"I just hope we don't get into trouble," Celia said, snuggling sleepily under the covers.

The girls had drifted off to sleep and Mandie was dreaming of home again when the singing she had heard the night before came suddenly into her dream. She blinked her eyes and realized she was not dreaming any longer; she was really hearing singing. She nudged Celia, who immediately sat up and listened.

"That's the same singing I heard last night," Celia whispered.

"That's what I heard too," Mandie replied, turning to get out of bed.

"Where are you going, Mandie?" Celia asked. She went over to where Mandie was quickly putting on a robe.

"To see if I can tell where it's coming from. Come on."

Celia grabbed her robe and followed Mandie as she silently opened the door to the hallway.

The two girls stopped in the hallway and listened. The singing seemed to come from the other end of the house. They crept down the dimly lit hallway. When they came to the heavy door dividing the east wing from the center section of the chalet, the singing grew louder.

"It sounds like someone in the west wing," Mandie whispered while they continued.

But when they passed through the doorway into the

west wing, the sound grew much fainter. The girls stopped for a moment.

"It's back that way," Mandie told Celia softly, leading the way back into the center section of the house.

When they paused in the hallway above the main stairs, the singing was more distinct.

"It must be around here somewhere," Mandie said, quietly opening doors from the hallway into rooms that they knew were unoccupied.

"Oh, this is aggravating!" Mandie exclaimed.

While she and Celia stood in the center of the landing, the singing suddenly stopped. Everything was absolutely quiet, not a sound anywhere.

"That beats all!" Mandie said in a loud whisper. "Now it stops before we can find out where it's coming from."

Even though the girls stood waiting for a few minutes, there was no more singing to be heard. Giving up, they went back to bed.

Mandie rolled over and said, "I think it came from the tower."

"I just don't know," Celia said. "It sounded to me like it was coming from down in the yard."

"How about waking me up if you hear it any more tonight?" Mandie asked. "And if I hear it I'll wake you. Tomorrow we'll talk to Jonathan."

The girls dropped off to sleep and Snowball curled up on their feet.

The house was quiet for the rest of the night.

Chapter 7 / Dangerous Plans

At the breakfast table the next morning, no one bothered to mention the fact that the Bagatelles were not present.

Mrs. Taft told the young people she had no plans for them for the day. "Y'all may do whatever you wish today," she said, "just behave yourselves. We came here to relax and rest, so that's what I think we ought to do."

"But we do need some exercise," Senator Morton said, taking a sip of his coffee. "Maybe we could all take a long walk."

Mandie sighed, looked at him, and said, "Maybe tomorrow, Senator Morton. I'd like to be lazy today."

"It's nice to be lazy once in a while," Jonathan said.

Uncle Ned looked around the table and asked, "I go visit friends of friends. Does Papoose like to go? We get pony cart." He smiled.

The young people looked interested, but Mandie,

thinking how long his visit might be, quickly declined, saying, "I don't think so, Uncle Ned. I don't even know these people you're going to visit."

"I not know people, but friends back home know people. Ask me visit."

Mandie wondered how his friends back home could have friends all the way across the ocean in Switzerland. But then Uncle Ned knew lots of important people, all the way up to the President of the United States. It might be an interesting visit, but she decided she'd better stay at the chalet and make plans with her friends for their search. After all, they would only be in this house a few days before they traveled on to Germany.

"Thank you, Uncle Ned, for asking me, but I'll just stay here today," Mandie told him politely.

As they all rose from the table after the meal, Mrs. Taft turned to the senator and said, "I believe a nice long walk would be invigorating. Shall we go?"

The senator smiled and agreed.

"Don't y'all get lost now," Mrs. Taft admonished the young people. "And be sure you are ready and waiting when it's time for the noon meal."

"Yes, ma'am," the three chorused.

Mandie with Snowball on his leash and her friends walked down to the stables with Uncle Ned as he went to get his horse. Jonathan had whispered that this might be a good time to get some rope while Eckart was busy saddling the Indian's horse.

Mandie and Celia kept talking to Uncle Ned and following Eckart around while he brought the horse in and put the saddle on. Jonathan disappeared.

Uncle Ned squeezed Mandie's small hand as he

mounted. "Papoose be good," he told her. "I not here to see. But Big God see. I be back before sunset."

"And *you* be good, Uncle Ned," Mandie teased as she waved and the old Indian rode off. Snowball ignored the activity, meowing and rubbing around his mistress's ankles.

Mandie and Celia turned to face Eckart after they saw Uncle Ned ride away. "That cat is not afraid of horses," he said.

"Oh, no, you see, Snowball was born on the farm where I lived with my father. We had horses," Mandie explained, as Snowball played with pebbles in the doorway of the stable. Her eyes darted around, trying to locate Jonathan. She hoped he had already taken some rope and gone back to the house with it.

When Eckart wasn't looking at Celia, she looked at Mandie and rolled her eyes toward the house. Mandie understood that Jonathan was gone.

"If you'd like to ride in the cart again, I would be happy to get it ready for you," Eckart offered, smiling at Mandie.

"Not right now, Eckart. Thanks anyway," said Mandie. "I think we'll go back to the house."

Before leaving, she decided to question him about the tale surrounding the tower. "Eckart, please tell us about the tower. We won't tell anyone, will we, Celia?"

Celia shook her head.

Eckart looked at Mandie silently for a moment and then at Celia before he finally spoke. "I am sorry, but I must honor my employers' wishes. I cannot discuss their private affairs. You understand that, don't you?"

"Yes, but this tale about the tower, whatever it is, is not exactly private business if the whole village knows about it," Mandie said.

"It is all right if you discuss it with some of the villagers, but all the servants here have been forbidden to talk of it," Eckart said. He turned and started back toward the stable. He stopped and added, "Whenever you wish to use the cart, please let me know. I sincerely hope you will enjoy your visit here. Now I must go back to work." With that, he went on inside the building.

Mandie and Celia looked at each other, then started walking back to the house.

"Maybe we should have gone with Uncle Ned," Mandie said. "Who knows, we might have met up with someone to talk to about the tower. No one here is going to tell us about it."

"Mandie, maybe we are meddling in the Thalers' private business," Celia said as they neared the house. "Have you thought about that?"

"Not really *meddling*, Celia, when everyone in the whole countryside is supposed to have heard about the tower. It's common knowledge," Mandie said. She saw Mrs. Taft and Senator Morton in the distance sitting on a bench amid a profusion of bright blooms. "There's Grandmother and the senator, over there. Come on. Let's hurry and find Jonathan before Grandmother changes her mind and decides to find something for us to do." She scooped up Snowball and ran up the steps to the door.

As the girls hurriedly entered the hallway, they saw the Bagatelles coming down the main stairway. Mandie stooped to busy herself with Snowball so she could see where they were going. The Bagatelles ignored the girls as they carried on their conversation in French and disappeared down the long corridor toward the parlor.

There was a soft "psst" from above and the girls looked up to see Jonathan standing at the top of the stairs. They quickly went up the steps.

"Did you get the rope?" Mandie asked in a whisper, in case someone else was around.

"Sure. I got lots of it—more than we'll need," Jonathan told the girls with a smile. "I hid it under my bed."

The girls laughed.

"Oh, you know, Jonathan," said Mandie, "we haven't had a chance to tell you, but we heard the singing again last night."

"You did? And you didn't call me?" Jonathan was clearly disappointed. "What did you do?"

"Celia and I walked around the house trying to decide which direction it was coming from, but we just couldn't tell," Mandie explained.

"I must have slept awfully sound, because I didn't hear it," Jonathan said, leading the way into the parlor at the top of the stairs. "Look, girls, please call me if you hear it again."

The girls agreed. Mandie put Snowball down and stooped to take off his leash. Suddenly she jumped up and excitedly told her friends, "I know! I know! I know where the singing was coming from—the tower!"

Celia and Jonathan looked at her in surprise and sat down on the settee.

"The tower? How do you know?" Jonathan asked.

"The tower is supposed to be haunted, remember? Mandie said. "There has to be some reason that everyone thinks it's haunted—something you can see, or hear, or something!"

"You're right," Jonathan agreed quickly.

"But, Mandie," Celia objected, "the singing didn't

sound like it was coming from the tower. I thought it sounded like someone in the yard."

"That could be because this house is so monstrous that everything echoes. The walls are so thick, and there are so many hallways and doors and everything, you never know where the sound is coming from," Mandie told her.

"Well, maybe," Celia said, evidently not completely convinced by Mandie.

"If we can get to the tower, I think we'll find the source of this singing," Mandie told her friends.

"And we'll do that tonight," Jonathan said.

"You mean we'll *try*," Mandie corrected him. "It may not be possible to cross the roof and get inside the tower."

"We can do it," Jonathan assured her.

"Just the same, I think we ought to keep on looking for some way to get into the tower," Mandie told him. "Just stop and think. This house was built with the tower in the original section, and there must have been some entrance into the tower back then. Otherwise, why build the tower? Besides, it has windows, and the windows have curtains. Where did they come from?"

"But the house could have been remodeled, Mandie, and the tower completely sealed off," Celia said.

"I don't agree with that," Mandie said. "For one thing, as far as I can tell, the curtains on the windows in the tower don't look old and dirty. They would be if there was no way to get inside and wash them now and then."

"The remodeling could have been done recently, perhaps when the Thalers bought it," Celia suggested.

"I still think there's a way in," Mandie insisted.

"You may be right, Mandie, and we can continue

looking, but I don't think we'll find any entrance to the tower—at least not from the house," Jonathan said.

"Well, what are we waiting for?" Mandie asked, standing up. "Pretty soon it'll be time to go downstairs and eat."

"Wait," Jonathan told her. "Let's get our plans settled for tonight first. That is, our plans if we don't find an entrance from the house."

"All right, but let's hurry," Mandie insisted.

"We can tie the rope around the beam between the windows, like we said," Jonathan said. "I'll grab the rope and swing out onto the roof, then work my way over to the chimney. I'll fasten the rope there, but I'll leave enough slack in it so you can grasp it here at the window and hold on to it while you follow."

"You mean like putting one hand in front of the other as I swing on the rope?" Mandie asked, sitting back down.

"Right," Jonathan replied. "It won't be as bad as it sounds, because your feet will still touch the roof as you swing forward, and I'll also tie a piece of rope around your waist just in case you should slip."

"And what are you going to be doing all this time?" Mandie asked.

"I'll wait for you when I get to the chimney," Jonathan said. "And then we can work our way to the window of the tower."

"And what if the window in the tower is locked?" Mandie asked.

"I'll carry a hammer in my belt and we'll just break the glass if necessary," Jonathan said confidently.

"But, Jonathan, we'd be destroying other people's property," Celia spoke up.

"I can always pay to have it fixed," Jonathan replied.

"But you won't have any money until your father

comes over to Europe unless you borrow it from the senator or us," Celia reminded him.

"I know, but I can always get money from somewhere," Jonathan said. "Now you, Celia, should wait down on the lawn below us and warn us if anyone comes along and sees what we're doing. You could start singing or something."

"And you'll have to stay pretty well hidden down there so nobody sees you. They'll wonder what you're doing out there alone at night if they see you," Mandie reminded her.

Celia sighed, "I sure hope we don't get caught."

"We won't go up there until we think everyone is in bed and asleep for the night," Jonathan assured her.

"But remember," said Mandie, "the observation room, where we have to go outside, is in the wing where Grandmother and Senator Morton are staying."

"But it's not close to their suites," Jonathan said.

Mandie stood up again and picked up Snowball as she put his leash back on. "Let's go up there and look things over now that we have plans made. I want to see if it looks possible," she said.

The three quietly made their way up to the observation room. They didn't want anyone to notice them. And they especially didn't want to run into the Bagatelles.

Arriving at the top of the stairs, they found the room empty.

Mandie pointed and asked, "You're talking about this beam here?" The wide beam stuck out on the outside of the window. All the windows seemed to have a similar beam for ornamental purposes.

Jonathan came to her side and leaned out the window. "Right," he said. "Now look out that way. See that chimney? I think I can swing over to it on a rope."

Mandie leaned out beside him. She could see a huge chimney some distance away. When she looked down, she realized how high up they were. It would be an awfully long drop to the yard from up here if they slipped and fell. For some reason she was nervous about the whole plan.

Celia, standing behind them, said, "I sure hope y'all don't fall or get hurt. It could be awfully dangerous."

That made up Mandie's mind. She would show Celia she was not afraid to take chances. Celia was always scared of everything.

"Oh, Celia, we're not going to fall or get hurt," Mandie told her. She turned to look at her friend and said, "You'll probably be in more danger down there alone in the dark by yourself. Are you sure you want to do it?"

"Of course, I'll do it, Mandie," Celia said quickly but nervously. "Don't worry about me."

"All right, it's all settled then," Mandie said. "Why don't we go look around in that room in the servants' quarters now?"

"But we've already been there twice. I don't see what we could hope to find," Jonathan said.

"Well, I really wanted to see if the Bagatelles are in there, and we could also look into some of the other rooms," Mandie said.

"I hope we don't run into Helga, not after she told us not to go into that part of the house again," Celia said.

"I think we can avoid her," Mandie said, opening the door and leading them down the narrow steps.

They didn't encounter anyone along the way. Once inside the servant's room, they closed the door.

"I just can't figure out what the Bagatelles were looking at when we saw them in here. They were standing by the window," Mandie said, going to look down into the yard. "And I just don't see anything worth staring at down there."

"I see one of the servants' cottages over there in the trees," Celia remarked, pointing down. "I believe it's the one Eckart said was unoccupied, isn't it?"

"I suppose so," Mandie said, following her gaze. "But why would they be staring at a vacant cottage? Remember they were saying something about they thought it could be done? What could be done, I wonder?"

"If we watch them long enough, we might find out," Jonathan said. "Let's go find them and see what they're doing."

The girls agreed, and as the three quietly left the room, they heard someone coming down the hallway around the corner. They quickly darted into a nearby room and watched through a crack in the door.

It was Helga! As they watched, she went into the empty room they had been in and closed the door.

"Quick! Let's get out of here!" Jonathan told the girls.

Mandie held Snowball tightly as they scurried down the hallway and through the dividing doors. They paused at the top of the main staircase.

"Should we check the strangers' suite to see if they're in there?" Mandie asked.

"Sure," Jonathan agreed.

"But let's be quiet," Celia said.

As they moved silently down the hallway near the Bagatelles' suite, they could hear the couple speaking in French. The young people slowed down and crept closer. They found the door standing open, so they peeked in. Through the doorway, they could see the man and woman doing something with a tall stand of some kind.

"What are they doing?" Mandie whispered in Jonathan's ear.

Jonathan motioned for them to back up so they could talk. They retreated down the hallway a short distance and Mandie asked, "What was that contraption the man was standing up?"

"That contraption was a tripod for a camera," Jonathan explained. "He was evidently setting up a camera."

Mandie was puzzled. "That's strange. What would he be doing with a camera like that?"

"Maybe they were going outside to take pictures," Celia suggested.

"Maybe, but why set up the stand inside the house?" Mandie wondered.

Suddenly they heard the Bagatelles leave their suite. The three looked down the hallway and saw the strangers start toward them. The man was carrying the tripod and the woman had a large black bag in her hand.

The young people slipped into an empty room nearby to avoid being seen.

"I don't think they saw us," Mandie whispered to her friends as they peeked around the slightly opened door.

"There they go," Jonathan said.

"Let's follow them," Mandie said.

They waited until the couple was far enough ahead, then the young people followed.

The Bagatelles went outside and around to the back of the chalet. There, as the young people watched from the bushes, the man set up the tripod and took a camera out of the bag his wife was carrying. "We're too close," he said.

They picked up everything and moved away from the house. He finally found a proper place and set up the camera aimed at the center part of the house.

"The tower! They're going to take a picture of the tower!" Mandie exclaimed.

Mandie was right. As the young people watched from behind the bushes, the strangers took a picture of the tower. Then they carefully returned the camera to the bag, picked up the tripod, and headed back around the house and through the front door. Mandie and her friends followed.

The three stopped in the yard as the Bagatelles went through the front door.

"Those people certainly do puzzle me," Mandie said, holding on to Snowball's leash as she let him down.

"Evidently they are interested in the tower, but why take one picture of it and then go back inside?" Jonathan said.

"I wonder what they are going to do next," Celia said.

"Well, I certainly hope they don't get in our way tonight when we go out on the roof," Mandie said, looking down the pathway at two approaching figures. "Here come Grandmother and Senator Morton. It must be time to eat."

"Did you definitely agree to try our plan tonight?" Jonathan asked quickly, before the adults drew too near.

"I suppose so," Mandie said. "Unless we find another way to get into the tower before tonight."

"We may not have time," Celia said. "Remember, Uncle Ned will be back sooner or later and he'll probably want to stay around us."

"We'll see," Mandie said.

Chapter 8 / The Villagers' Tales

During the noon meal the young people were relieved that Mrs. Taft had nothing planned for them during the afternoon except for tea. Mrs. Taft and Senator Morton planned to take the pony cart out for a ride and asked the three young people to go, but Mandie and her friends declined. The adults cautioned them to behave while they were gone.

"We are going into the little village near here to look for a church," Mrs. Taft explained as they rose from their seats around the table. "Tomorrow is Sunday and we need to go to a service somewhere. According to Mrs. Hedgewick, the Thalers attend one of the village churches."

Mandie quickly looked at her friends. If they went to the village with the adults, they might have a chance to talk to someone about the "haunted" tower. There was a silent understanding among the three.

"We didn't know you were going into the village, Grandmother," Mandie told her. "I think I would like to see what's there."

"So would I," Jonathan added.

"And I think it would be interesting to meet some of the local people," Celia said.

"All right, that's fine," Mrs. Taft told them. "Y'all have about fifteen minutes to get freshened up while the senator has the cart brought around. And, girls, you will of course wear your bonnets. The sun is strong enough today to put some freckles on that fair skin. Hurry now."

The girls rushed upstairs for their bonnets and Jonathan went with the senator to get the cart.

"This might give us a chance to ask someone about the tower," Mandie said, running up the stairs with Celia to their suite.

"That's exactly what I was thinking, too," Celia said.

"But we shouldn't let Grandmother or the senator hear what we're asking if we find anyone to talk to," Mandie said.

They rushed into their suite and found Snowball curled up sound asleep in the middle of Mandie's bed. He sleepily opened one eye to peer at his mistress and closed it again as he rolled up tighter.

"Are you taking Snowball?" Celia asked. She ran into her bedroom, fetched her bonnet, and returned to Mandie's room.

"I don't know," Mandie said, thoughtfully looking at the kitten. "He's asleep and he might be a lot of trouble if I take him. However, the fresh air would do him good."

The girls stood before the mirror on the dresser and hastily put on their bonnets.

"I'll help you take care of him if you want to take him, Mandie," Celia offered.

"All right. Thanks," Mandie replied. She bent across the bed and scooped up the white kitten.

Snowball yawned, stretched in her arms, and looked up at his mistress. Celia took his leash from a nearby table and hooked it to his harness while Mandie held him.

"Let's go," Mandie said, putting Snowball up on her shoulder as they hurried back downstairs.

They were soon on their way to the village along a hard, packed dirt road that led in a different direction from the road they had ridden on from the town that first night.

"If y'all have never been to visit the Thalers before, how do you know the way to the village?" Mandie asked Senator Morton, who was driving.

He smiled at her and said, "The housekeeper and Eckart explained that there is only one road into the village, and this is it."

"Oh, I see," Mandie replied, holding tight to Snowball as they bounced along.

"How far away is this village?" Jonathan asked from the back seat.

"Twenty or thirty minutes drive is the way Eckart explained it," Senator Morton replied. He held on to the reins and said, "This is where they go for supplies. There's a doctor in the village and a few shops."

"The village is quite old," Mrs. Taft told them. "Some of the buildings were probably built over a hundred— or maybe two hundred—years ago."

"It sounds interesting," Mandie said, becoming excited about the prospect of seeing the local architecture. She was always fascinated by the age of everything in Europe. Most of the houses had been built before the United States became a country.

They soon came to small, old houses scattered along the way. As the settlement grew thicker, they saw people walking along the road and children playing. Some of the buildings were large structures of old stones. Some were well-kept and some in a sad disrepair. Steeples of churches rose above the mass of shops and dwellings, and the young people began counting the churches.

"I see at least six steeples," Mandie remarked as they bumped over the cobblestones of the main village street. "Why are there so many churches in such a small village?"

"Switzerland has several different nationalities and several different religions. Most people here are Protestant or Catholic, but there are many other religious groups," Senator Morton explained. He drew the cart up in front of a small stone church and continued, "Every different denomination must have its own place to worship. You'll understand as we look around."

They alighted from the cart and began their tour of the village. The local people secretly stared at them, but tried to give the impression that they were ignoring the Americans. Mandie noticed this right away and drew her friends' attention to it.

"Everyone is curious about us, but they don't want us to see them staring," Mandie whispered to Celia and Jonathan as she walked along between them. She had to hold Snowball tightly in her arms because he struggled to get down.

"So I noticed," Celia said, softly.

"We don't have to whisper," Jonathan said. "I'm pretty sure no one can hear us because they're keeping so far away from us."

Mrs. Taft and Senator Morton stopped ahead of them. Mrs. Taft turned back to say, "Y'all come on. We're going into this church." She pointed to a small stone building in front of them.

The young people hurried on and followed the adults through the arched doorway of the building. The interior was dark except for sunlight coming through a few narrow slits of windows. Several stone benches sat in front of a tiny altar, which was covered by a brightly colored embroidered cloth. There was a small door in a far corner. The floor was made of stone, but was spotless.

Mandie shivered as she looked around. "Whew! It feels cold in here!"

"Yes, and imagine having to sit on one of those cold stone benches through a long sermon," Celia replied.

Mrs. Taft walked around the room with the senator and then remarked, "I don't believe there is anyone about."

"Maybe the minister lives in the cottage next door," Senator Morton suggested.

"We'll go find out," Mandie quickly told her grandmother.

Mrs. Taft looked at her granddaughter and said, "We should all go."

"We could have a moment of silent prayer here while the young people go ask about the minister," the senator told her.

Mrs. Taft smiled at him and said, "You're right." She turned back to Mandie. "You may go next door now, nowhere else. And you are to come back immediately. This is a strange place to us and I don't want anyone to get lost." Then she added, "And, Amanda, whatever you do, don't let that cat get loose. We'd never find him."

"Yes, ma'am," chorused the three young people as they rushed out the church door.

Without discussing the matter among themselves, they immediately ran to the small stone cottage next to the church. The front door was standing open and they could see inside. The furnishings were old and meager, and it seemed to have only one room. An old woman with a book in her lap dozed in a chair.

Mandie knocked on the door frame and called, "Excuse me, ma'am, but we are looking for the minister of the church next door."

The old woman woke with a startled gasp as she saw the three standing in the doorway. She blinked her eyes and pushed herself to her feet using the arms of the chair. Toddling toward them, she stared at Snowball in Mandie's arms.

The young people smiled at her, but she stood silently before them, staring.

"Does the minister of the church next door live here?" Jonathan asked.

The woman looked at him, but still didn't reply.

Jonathan quickly repeated what he said, this time in French, and the woman's face brightened in understanding. She responded in French. Mandie and Celia squirmed as they listened to the conversation, unable to understand a word that was being said.

Finally Jonathan turned back to the girls and said, "She says he does live here, but he is out visiting some sick parishioners. Today is Saturday, and that is the day he makes his rounds in the country."

"Quick, Jonathan," Mandie said breathlessly, "ask her if she knows anything about the tower in the Thalers' house. Quick!"

Jonathan spoke again in French to the woman and she frowned. She replied in a slower, more emphatic voice. Mandie and Celia watched and tried to decipher some of the French.

When the woman paused, Jonathan told the girls, "She says everyone knows about the tower. Many, many years ago, before anyone living now was ever born, a beautiful young maiden lived with her parents in the chalet. The girl fell in love with a young man who was beneath her family's station in life and they forbid the marriage—"

Mandie interrupted excitedly, "And what happened?"

Jonathan smiled mischievously and said, "I'm trying to tell you, if you'll only give me time." He paused to look at the girls.

"All right, all right, go on," Mandie told him.

"Yes, please continue," Celia said.

"The woman says the young maiden's heart was broken and she tried to run away. Her parents caught her and locked her up in the tower. Soon after that, the girl jumped from a tower window and killed herself," Jonathan explained.

Mandie and Celia both gasped as their eyes grew big. "That's just what Uncle Ned told us!" said Mandie.

The old woman stood watching them.

"Well, what makes people think it's haunted? What is it that they see or hear, or what's the rest of the story?" Mandie asked excitedly.

Jonathan asked the woman about the tower again. She replied, and he turned back to the girls and translated. "She says for years now there has been singing in the middle of the night, and people believe it is the spirit of the dead girl."

"Singing!" Mandie and Celia both exclaimed.

"Probably what you girls heard," Jonathan said with a big smile.

"Jonathan, ask her if the singing comes from the tower," Mandie told him. "Has anyone ever investigated this tale?"

Jonathan asked the woman the questions in French and, after she had answered, explained to the girls, "Yes, different people have investigated over many years, but no one has ever been able to discover the source of the singing. The last owners had lived there for years and years and, as far as anyone knows, they never used the tower. And now that the Thalers own the place, the villagers are waiting to see if the tower's secret will be solved."

"Oh, Jonathan, please thank this lady for us," Mandie said. "And tell her if we can find out where the singing is coming from we'll let her know."

Jonathan translated Mandie's words to the woman and her face brightened with a smile. She reached to touch a stray wisp of blonde hair escaping from under Mandie's bonnet as she said something to Jonathan.

"She wishes us luck. For many, many years now no

one has been able to solve the mystery," Jonathan said.

"Mandie, we'd better go back to the church," Celia reminded her.

The three smiled at the woman and turned to leave. Then Mandie stopped. "Jonathan, you'd better ask her the minister's name and what time his service will be tomorrow. Grandmother will want to know."

Jonathan asked her and as they left he said, "His name is Reverend Claude Saverne. The lady is his mother and the service is around eleven o'clock tomorrow, depending on how long it takes some of the people to come in from the country."

"Remember to tell Grandmother that," Mandie said, and then excitedly added, "I told you the singing was coming from the tower. I could tell by the sound."

"Wait a minute," Jonathan told her. "The lady didn't say it was coming from the tower for sure. She said some people *thought* it was coming from the tower. No one has ever proved anything."

"We will," Mandie told her friends. "We'll solve this mystery for the villagers. Evidently they believe in ghosts and things like that, but I know better. There has to be some explanation for the singing, and I'm going to find out what it is."

The young people hurried back into the church and found the adults sitting on one of the cold stone benches in front of the altar. When they turned and saw the three enter, they stood up.

Mandie rushed up to her grandmother and said, "The minister does live next door." Snowball squirmed in her arms and she let him down to walk on his leash.

"And we spoke with his mother. He's out visiting the

sick," the boy explained. "Service is tomorrow around eleven o'clock or as soon as the country people get in."

"And his name is Reverend Claude Saverne," Celia added.

"Then this is the right church," Mrs. Taft said to the senator. He agreed.

"We'll all come to the service here tomorrow," Mrs. Taft told the young people. "And it's cold in here because of all this stone, so I would suggest that you dress accordingly."

"I'll bring my shawl and sit on it," Mandie whispered to Celia.

Jonathan, overhearing the remark, smiled mischievously at the girls. "I might just bring a pillow to sit on," he teased.

Mrs. Taft touched Mandie on the shoulder and said, "Pick up that cat, dear. We're going to walk around outside."

Mandie tried to pick up Snowball, but he played with her and pulled on the leash. She gathered in the leash and caught him. "Snowball, maybe I'll let you walk outside," Mandie told him.

The adults went on ahead of them and Mandie whispered to Celia and Jonathan, "If we get a chance, let's talk to somebody else here in this village about that tower."

Her friends agreed.

The village only had one narrow street running through its entire length. Small alleyways crisscrossed here and there between the closely built cottages. Upon Senator Morton's suggestion, they explored the byways. At the end of one lane they found a blacksmith at work.

As they approached the man and his shop, Mandie remarked, "I know what he is. He's the village blacksmith, just like the blacksmith we have back home."

"Smart, aren't you?" Jonathan teased. "That happens to be what the shingle over his shop says."

"But it's evidently in French, because I can't read it," Mandie said defensively. Then she stopped and looked at Jonathan. "Why, I doubt that you've ever seen a blacksmith, since you live in New York."

"Oh, but I've traveled a lot, remember?" Jonathan replied. "I will have to admit I've never seen a blacksmith at work."

Mandie immediately caught up with her grandmother and asked, "Grandmother, could we stop and watch the blacksmith work over there? Jonathan's never seen one."

Mrs. Taft agreed.

As they approached the shop they could feel the heat from the huge fire the blacksmith had going. The man looked up at them for an instant and silently went back to his work. The young people crowded close to watch as pieces of iron were heated in the fire and then hammered out into horseshoes on the anvil nearby. The blacksmith occasionally worked a large bellows to keep the fire hot. By opening the top of the bellows like a fan, air rushed inside, and when it was closed, the air came out of a nozzle at the bottom and blew the fire into flames.

Jonathan edged closer and asked the man a question in French. The man looked up at him and, having heard the group speaking, said, "I speak English."

Mandie and Celia smiled and drew a breath of relief.

Here at last was someone they could talk to. Mrs. Taft and Senator Morton had wandered over to a small shop nearby.

"I'm sorry. I'm so used to other people not understanding English," Jonathan told the man. "I was just asking how many horses you normally shoe."

"All the horses for all the people everywhere," the man replied, waving his strong arms around. "I am the only smithy in this part of the country." He looked at the young people. "You are Americans?"

"Yes. How did you know?" Mandie asked.

"Because you speak American English," the man said, smiling at her.

Mandie quickly looked around to be sure her grandmother was not in hearing distance, then she asked the man, "Do you know anything about the story of the tower at the Thalers' house? We're visiting there."

"Story? And a story it be!" the man replied, wiping the sweat from his face. "Alas, the poor lass was not allowed to marry her love and her dear little heart was broken in twain. Now she tells the world about it with her song of sorrow."

Mandie instantly detected an odd accent, but before she could say anything, Jonathan spoke up, "You are Irish, aren't you? You have a lilt in your words like an Irishman."

"Sure I am," the man said proudly. "My mither did bring me to this country when I was a wee babe. This was my father's country. And I make it mine. But one day I'll cross the water again and see my mitherland before I give up this life on earth, the Lord willing."

"Irish!" Mandie exclaimed. "We're going to travel to

Ireland before we return home if we have time. I am also part Irish—and the other part is Cherokee Indian."

"Indian!" the man exclaimed. "You do not look like an Indian. But you do look Irish with those smiling blue eyes, lass." He gave her a big grin.

"Amanda," Mrs. Taft called from across the lane. "We should walk on now."

"Yes, Grandmother," Mandie replied. She quickly stepped forward and put out a small white hand to the man. "I'd like to shake the hand of a real Irishman, sir."

The man grasped her dainty hand in his big strong one and said, "Now don't you be atrying to solve the mystery in that tower. 'Tis bad luck to meddle in such things. And if the people who did meddle in it were alive to tell you, you'd be knowing that only harm came to them."

"What!" Mandie asked in surprise. "Harm came to anyone trying to solve the mystery? But you know there's got to be some reasonable explanation for it. There's no such thing as ghosts."

"Ah, but there be, miss," the man said. "You say Irish blood flows through your veins and you don't believe in such things? When you get to Ireland, don't let the people know that. They won't claim you as a daughter of their land."

"Amanda!" Mrs. Taft called again. "We have to go."

"Yes, Grandmother," Mandie replied, and quickly said to the man, "I'm going to prove the story is just a tale. Wait and see. Thank you and goodbye." She threw the man a kiss as she ran to catch up with her grandmother and the others.

Mandie didn't know much about her Irish heritage,

but she had never heard of anyone really believing in ghosts as the smithy did. And she didn't believe harm would come to a person just for investigating the story of the tower. She'd prove him wrong.

Chapter 9 / Trouble in the Night

Uncle Ned had not returned by supper time that night, and the Bagatelles still didn't come to the table but had trays taken to their suite. The young people were hungry after their visit in the village, and they were also in a hurry to get away from the adults so they could discuss the afternoon's events and their adventure for that night. Snowball had been left with a maid who would feed him and then put him in Mandie's room.

"I think we should all retire early tonight," Mrs. Taft remarked as she cut the piece of meat on her plate. "We've had an invigorating day and we should all sleep well."

"Early, Grandmother?" Mandie asked across the table. "How early?"

"I'd say nine o'clock for you young people," Mrs. Taft said. "We'll have to be up early to get finished with the morning's details and get to church on time."

"Nine o'clock," Mandie repeated, as she laid down her fork. "But Grandmother, Uncle Ned isn't even back yet. Shouldn't we wait up until he gets back?"

"Well, dear, it looks as though he is staying longer than he had planned," Mrs. Taft replied. "However, he is a grown man and capable of taking care of himself. I don't see any reason to wait up for him."

Mandie looked at Celia and Jonathan. She knew what they were thinking. Uncle Ned had to be home and in bed before they could try to get to the tower across the roof. Otherwise he might interfere with their plans.

"We could go to our rooms and write in our journals," Celia suggested. "We haven't been keeping up with them."

"I suppose so," said Mandie, "but I've decided that I'm not the kind of person who can set a routine of writing everything down. I always forget or it's just not convenient when I want to record something."

"Too disorganized," Jonathan said.

"So what? I think being organized would take the fun out of everything," Mandie replied. "I wouldn't have time to solve all the mysteries we run into."

"Amanda," Mrs. Taft said, as her attention was drawn to this remark. "You are not planning any escapades I hope. You are getting old enough now that I expect you to act like the young lady you are. And speaking of writing, have you written to your mother lately? And you too, Celia. I'm sure both of them are anxious to hear from y'all."

"I sent my mother a letter when we first got to Europe, Grandmother, but I will write another one tonight,"

Mandie said, picking up her fork to continue eating.

"And I will too," Celia promised. "I've already mailed her three letters since we left home."

"What about you, Jonathan? Have you written to your father since we contacted him?" Mrs. Taft asked.

"No, ma'am, I haven't," Jonathan admitted reluctantly. "I don't think I've ever written a letter to my father, and he is always too busy to write to me. He stays in touch with the schools where I live."

"My boy, take some advice from an older man," Senator Morton spoke up. "Sit down and write a few lines to your father. That could change the entire relationship between you two."

"I wouldn't know what to write because I hardly know my father," Jonathan replied, fiddling with his silverware.

"That's because neither one of you has made the first effort," Senator Morton said. "If you don't know what to write, just sit down and scribble a few lines about your experiences since you met up with us, what we've been doing and seeing. I'm sure he'd be interested in knowing that."

Jonathan cleared his throat nervously and said, "I'll try."

"That's all it takes to do anything, Jonathan—just trying," Mandie encouraged him. "You never know what the outcome of anything will be until you try."

"I have an idea," Celia spoke up. "Why don't the three of us get together tonight and discuss our travels and help each other write our letters."

"That is a good idea, Celia," Mrs. Taft said. "The three of you may use the little parlor at the top of the stairs to write your letters. But I want all of you in your rooms by nine o'clock."

"Yes, ma'am," the three replied as they looked at each other. After the meal they all retired to the main parlor and discussed what they had done on their journey and what they planned to do.

"We'll be leaving here to visit the Baroness Geissler in Germany," Mrs. Taft reminded the young people.

The three young people looked alarmed.

"When?" Mandie asked quickly.

"In a few days," Mrs. Taft said. "I was hoping the Thalers would get back home before we left, but it doesn't look like they will. Mrs. Hedgewick told me today that Mrs. Thalers' mother is no better."

"Her mother lives in Germany and we are going to Germany," Mandie spoke up. "Maybe we could visit Mrs. Thaler at her mother's when we go to see the baroness."

Mrs. Taft smiled at her granddaughter and said, "Unfortunately, dear, we couldn't do that. Germany is large, and the baroness doesn't live anywhere near Mrs. Thalers' mother. We'll just have to come back here next time we come to Europe to visit with the Thalers."

"We could wait a few more days for Mrs. Thaler to come home," Senator Morton said. "We have an open invitation to visit the baroness."

"Maybe," Mrs. Taft replied. "We don't want to waste time, though, because we have lots of other places to travel to before we return home."

The grandfather clock struck eight and Mandie immediately rose.

"We'd better go write those letters if we're going to be in our rooms by nine o'clock," she said, looking at her friends.

"Yes, dear, y'all go ahead and be sure you're in bed by nine o'clock," Mrs. Taft reminded.

After good nights were said, the young people raced to their rooms for paper and pens and met in the parlor at the top of the stairs.

The three didn't waste time on conversation, but hastily scribbled their letters. As they folded them up and put them into envelopes, Jonathan smiled and said, "I managed to write one page."

"That's better than nothing," Mandie said, quickly licking her envelope.

"I can think of so much to say to my mother I have trouble stopping once I get started," Celia remarked as she sealed her letter in the envelope.

"I understand if we leave these letters on the table in the front hallway downstairs, the servants will mail them for us," Jonathan said.

"If y'all will give me yours, I'll take them down," Celia said, rising.

"We need a last-minute conference before we go to our rooms," Jonathan said.

"Right," Mandie agreed. "Remember we have to listen out for Uncle Ned to come back. And we have to watch out for the Bagatelles. They are always roaming around the house and we might run into them. I hope they're not in the observation room when we go up there."

"We know your grandmother and Senator Morton are retiring at nine o'clock, and the servants here seem to disappear after supper every night, so that's most of the people out of the way," Jonathan remarked. "Why don't we meet here in this parlor at ten o'clock?"

"That's a good idea, because we don't want to be up too late," Mandie agreed. "You know Grandmother said we had to get up early to go to church."

"And I don't want to stand down there in the yard by myself at too late an hour," Celia said.

"All right, we meet here at ten. Don't forget," Jonathan told the girls.

"Wait for me till I take these letters down," Celia said, rushing out of the room.

"I hope no one sees Celia in the yard at that hour," Mandie remarked to Jonathan after her friend had left the room.

"And I hope she doesn't panic, all alone in the dark," Jonathan added.

Celia quickly returned and the three went to their suites.

"I think we'd better put out the lights, just in case my grandmother comes to check on us or has the maid do it," Mandie said, reaching for Snowball who was curled up asleep in the middle of the bed. "Sorry, Snowball, but we've got to turn down the bed."

"And we'd better get into bed too," Celia added.

"But with our clothes on?" Mandie asked. "I don't want to have to undress and then dress again to go out on the roof." She set Snowball on the carpet.

Celia helped Mandie turn down the covers on the big bed and suggested, "Let's leave that small lamp on in the sitting room."

"All right, that way we can see the clock to know when it's ten o'clock," Mandie said, plumping up a pillow.

She and Celia jumped into bed and pulled the covers up to hide their clothes in case someone came in. Snowball immediately bounced up on their feet and curled up to go back to sleep.

"Don't forget to listen for Uncle Ned," Mandie reminded her friend. "I'm not sure whether we'll be able to hear him come in and go in his room or not."

"Mandie, poke me if I start dozing off," Celia said.

"We can talk in whispers so we don't get too sleepy," Mandie said softly.

"Do you think the people in Ireland really believe in ghosts, like that blacksmith said?" Celia asked in a whisper.

"I don't know. Maybe that man was just joking," Mandie replied. "Besides, he has evidently never been back to Ireland since his mother brought him over here as a baby. He can't know a whole lot about the country."

"But his mother was Irish, and she would have taught him what she believed," Celia reminded her.

"I know," Mandie said. "I've always heard people say the Irish are superstitious, but I've never really thought about it. There is an old lady who's Irish living near my father's house, and I know she used to say things like 'if your nose itches company is coming,' 'if your hand itches you're going to get money,' and 'if a black cat crosses your path you'll have bad luck if you continue on unless you turn your hat around backwards,' and all that kind of stuff."

"Oh, I've heard things like that," Celia agreed, "but I didn't know they were supposed to be Irish sayings."

"I don't know where they originated. One time I thought maybe they came from the Indians. You know, some of my Cherokee kinpeople have some strong beliefs in those same superstitions," Mandie whispered.

"Mandie, listen. I hear someone," Celia said softly. She sat up in bed to listen.

Mandie quickly crept out of bed and went to open the hall door just a crack. She got a glimpse of the Bagatelles as they went into their suite.

Mandie closed the door and ran to jump back in bed. "It was just the Bagatelles going to their suite," she told Celia.

"At least we know where they are," Celia whispered.

The girls lay still, listening for any other sounds. A few minutes later they heard a door open and close softly. Mandie jumped up again, but this time Mandie didn't see anyone when she peeked out into the hall.

"That had to be Uncle Ned," she said as she got back in bed.

"What do you think you'll find in the tower if you can get in from the roof?" Celia asked quietly.

"I have no idea, but there's got to be something in there, some reason the tower is closed. Mrs. Saverne said the people locked that girl in the tower so she couldn't run away. Maybe it's like a bedroom in there," Mandie said. "The girl had to have some kind of furniture to live in the tower."

"It's probably so old it's real dirty and falling apart," Celia said, "since this was all supposed to have happened before anyone living now was ever born. That's a long time ago. I looked around the village and saw some real old people."

"Celia, I just thought of something," Mandie exclaimed, sitting up in bed. "That minister's mother only speaks French. Do you suppose the minister will give his sermon in French? We won't be able to understand a word."

Celia giggled and said, "That would be funny. Either your grandmother, the senator, or Jonathan will have to tell us afterwards what the man said."

"But that blacksmith speaks English. I wonder if he goes to that church," Mandie said.

"Your grandmother said the Thalers are German and they go to that church," Celia reminded her.

"The languages are such a conglomeration here, I just don't know what he'll do," Mandie said. "If they sing hymns that we know, we can always sing in English while they're singing in French, I suppose."

Celia giggled again. "Now that would be funny," she whispered.

The girls talked on about different things. Mandie kept straining to see the clock every now and then. Finally when it was ten minutes till ten, she threw back the covers and got out of bed. Celia followed. They quickly threw the blanket back up over their pillows and left it rumpled.

"If anyone glances in here in the darkness they'll probably think we're in bed," Mandie declared with satisfaction as she looked at the bed. Snowball moved around, looked at his mistress, and decided to curl back up on the bed.

"And you, Snowball, have got to stay here," she told the kitten as she patted his head.

The girls straightened their wrinkled clothes and quietly hurried down the hall to meet Jonathan in the small parlor at the top of the stairs.

"Right on time," Jonathan greeted them as they

carefully opened the door. He held up a large coil of rope. "This ought to be plenty to reach across the roof."

"I hope so," Mandie said, looking at the rope. "Did you remember to bring a hammer?"

"Right here." He patted his belt where he had stuck a small hammer. "I took it from the stables tonight after everyone had gone to bed."

The girls gasped. "You've already been outside?" Mandie asked.

"Sure. The moon is shining so we should be able to see up on the roof," he said.

"That means you'll definitely have to stand in the shadow of the bushes down there, Celia, or someone might look out and see you," Mandie reminded her.

"Yes," Celia said, nervously.

"Let's go outside with Celia to see where she'll be and then we can come back inside and go up to the observation room," Mandie said.

"Yes, we have to be sure she's in a place where she can see the roof," Jonathan said. He pushed the rope under the settee in the room. "I'll leave that here and get it on the way back. Let's go."

The three crept softly down the dark staircase and quietly opened the front door. They stayed near the house in the shadow of the shrubbery just in case someone happened to look out a window.

"This way," Jonathan whispered, leading the way down the slope at the back of the chalet. Then he stopped and looked back up at the house. "This should be all right. You can see the windows of the observation room up there." He pointed to the room where he and Mandie would be and said, "And the chimney is over there, and then the tower."

Mandie looked around and walked over to a huge oak tree. "If you stand behind this tree, Celia, you can look around it and see the roof. If anyone comes by you can hide behind the big trunk," she said.

Celia did as Mandie suggested. She nervously looked around and said, "Y'all please hurry. I don't want to stay down here too long. It's just plain spooky this time of the night."

"All right, we'll hurry," Mandie promised. "Now don't forget to start singing if you see anyone in the yard here. If anyone hears singing they'll probably just think it's the singing that comes from the ghost, or whatever you want to call it, up in the tower. Watch out for us."

"I will," Celia promised. Mandie and Jonathan turned to hurry back into the house.

Jonathan got the rope from the parlor and they quietly crept up the steps to the observation room.

They didn't see or hear anyone. The moon was shining brightly through the windows in the room, and Jonathan quickly walked over to the beam and fastened the end of the rope securely to it. Then he tied another rope to the beam and wrapped the other end around Mandie's waist.

"That's for safety, just in case you slip. You see, you'll still be anchored to the beam here," Jonathan quietly explained. "And I'll do the same for myself." He fastened another rope to the beam and around his waist. He picked up the coil of the first rope and slung it over his shoulder.

"Please be careful," Mandie whispered.

"You too," Jonathan said softly, stepping out the French window. "When I get to the chimney you follow me as soon as I get the rope tied to it."

Mandie bent out the window to watch as Jonathan slowly made his way toward the chimney. She could see him swing out on the rope and then swing back onto the roof. He tried this several times before he was able to gain footing on the slanted roof. Then he lay down and wormed his way to the chimney. He threw the rope around it and tied it fast, then he looked back for Mandie.

Mandie thought it really looked pretty easy. She wasn't too frightened with the prospect of hanging on to a rope that high up and working her way over to where Jonathan was waiting. She looked down into the yard and barely made out Celia standing there in the darkness. Then she took a deep breath, grasped the rope Jonathan had just tied from the beam to the chimney and stepped out the window.

"Oh, goodness!" she exclaimed to herself, as her feet dangled in the air. "I've got to do this fast!"

She moved one hand and then the other as she worked her way along the rope toward the chimney. "If I can just get my feet on the roof," she grunted. Finally she felt the roof under her feet. She saw Jonathan watching from beside the chimney, and then she tried to look down to be sure Celia was still there.

As she held on to the rope with one hand, she tried to straighten her skirts so she could see below. She suddenly lost her grasp and felt herself falling toward the edge of the roof.

She gasped, but almost lost her breath when the next moment the rope around her waist jerked her up short against the side of the chalet below the windows.

"Oh, please help me!" she cried in a subdued voice as she tried to swing over to see where Jonathan was. She realized she was below the roof and completely out of Jonathan's sight. The rope seemed to have tightened around her waist and was cutting into her sides. Now and then her feet would brush against the wall of the chalet as she swung on the rope tied around her waist. She desperately tried to wiggle around and catch the rope with her hands to get the weight off her waist.

Suddenly she felt the rope give a little. She seemed to drop a little bit farther down.

"The rope is coming undone on the window beam," she cried to herself. "I'm going to fall to the ground and break my neck. Oh, dear God, please help me!"

She grew dizzy and felt herself fainting away.

Chapter 10 / Celia's Bravery

Mandie heard a voice saying, "Wake up, you silly girl." She blinked her eyes and realized she was talking to herself. She could remember falling from the roof, and the pain around her waist was still there, so she knew she was still hanging at the end of her rope.

"What time I am afraid I will put my trust in Thee," she quoted her favorite Bible verse. She believed she would be rescued, but staring at the ground from so far up didn't provide much comfort.

Another voice came from above her. It sounded like Jonathan, but she knew Jonathan was over at the chimney waiting for her. "Mandie, put your hands flat against the wall of the house and push up with your feet when I pull on the rope."

It was Jonathan! She tried to do as he said and she got a glimpse of him leaning over the edge of the roof, looking down at her. She was dangling against the wall of the house, but the rope around her waist threw her off balance.

"Oh, Jonathan, please help me," she called.

"I'm trying, but you've got to do what I say," Jonathan replied. "Now swing around and put your hands flat against the wall of the house. When I pull on the rope that's around your waist, you push up with your feet. Make like you're walking up the side of the house when the rope tightens. Ready now?"

Mandie twisted around and pressed the palms of her bruised hands against the stone wall. "Ready," she replied with a groan. She felt the rope tighten around her waist and almost cried out in pain, but she remembered that Jonathan had told her to push up with her feet. Finally managing to right herself against the wall, she pushed her feet with all her might in an effort to climb the wall. The rope tightened again as Jonathan pulled, but she didn't seem to move an inch upward.

"Just keep pushing up every time I pull on the rope," Jonathan called down to her.

She kept pushing upward with her feet and Jonathan kept pulling on the rope, but she wasn't moving any closer to safety. Never had she been so frightened in her life. She could see herself ending up in a pile on the ground below if she didn't get up soon.

"Mandie, hold on," another voice called down to her. "I'm going to help Jonathan pull the rope."

Mandie twisted around enough to look up. To her amazement, Celia was leaning over the edge of the roof looking at her. Her dear friend had overcome her fear of heights enough to come to her rescue.

"Come on, Mandie, get going," she told herself.

"You can do it. If Celia can get up the nerve to walk out on a roof, you certainly can manage to climb back up onto that roof."

As Jonathan and Celia pulled on the rope, Mandie gave a push for all she was worth. She felt herself being pulled over the edge and up onto the roof beside her friends. Her eyes filled with tears as Celia embraced her.

"Now we have to get back to the window of the observation room," Jonathan told them. "Mandie, your rope is still tied to the beam and so are Celia's and mine. Would you be able to hold tightly to the rope and pull yourself back up to the window? Just lie down and crawl as you pull on the rope, like I did when I went to the chimney, remember?"

"I'm sure I can—oh, Jonathan, I'm so sorry," Mandie said, trying to wipe the tears from her face as the three lay there on the roof. But she quickly realized that she must follow Jonathan's instructions and forget her earlier carelessness. She turned over on her stomach and started pulling herself up by the rope.

Celia came along behind her. Jonathan waited and watched in case the girls needed help.

"You're doing fine, Mandie," Celia whispered. "I'm right behind you in case you slip. We're getting close."

Mandie was so nervous she couldn't speak. When she finally reached the beam of the window and dropped into the observation room, she sat on the floor shaking.

Celia quickly put her arm around her. "Mandie, let's go to our room and get in bed. Are you all right? Can you walk?"

Jonathan had come in behind them and was kneeling by the girls.

"Mandie, I'm sorry. It was all my fault. I made such big, dangerous plans," Jonathan apologized. "I should have had more sense. I hope you're not hurt too bad."

Mandie looked at her friends and tried to speak, but her teeth chattered. She kept taking deep breaths and telling herself to quit being such a baby.

Jonathan and Celia untied all the ropes and coiled them up. They helped Mandie to her feet. She felt wobbly at first, but then she looked at her friends' worried expressions and managed a faint smile.

"Don't worry. I'm not hurt, just scared," she managed to say, her voice shaky.

The three got up and started for the stairs. They silently crept down the stairway and to their rooms without seeing anyone. At the door of their suite, Mandie, who was more stable on her feet now, turned to Jonathan and said, "I'm sorry, Jonathan."

"We'll talk about it in the morning. I'm just glad you're all right. You girls get to bed now," Jonathan said. He waited for Celia to open their door and then he turned back toward his suite.

As soon as the girls got to Mandie's bedroom, Mandie fell into bed with her clothes on and Celia did the same. After an adventure like she'd had, she was almost as shaky as Mandie.

"Good night, Celia, and thanks," Mandie mumbled as she relaxed in the big bed. Snowball rearranged himself, concerned only about being rudely pushed aside.

"Good night, Mandie," Celia replied. "I hope you sleep well." They both drifted off to sleep.

Sometime later Mandie dreamed that someone was singing. Then she slowly came awake and realized the singing was real and not in her dream. She started to get out of bed, but she hurt everywhere and decided it wasn't worth the effort. Tonight she wouldn't try to find the source of the singing. She dozed back to sleep.

The next time she woke, Celia was standing by the bed and shaking her. "Mandie, we should get up. We have to go to church this morning, remember?"

"Go to church? Oh, yes, that's right." Her grandmother had told them to be up early. They were all going into the village to the little church they had visited the day before. She rubbed her eyes and sat up. Every muscle seemed to be sore and aching. She looked at her hands. They were scratched and bruised.

"Celia, my grandmother is going to see all these scratches and bruises on my hands and ask what I've been up to," Mandie exclaimed.

"Aren't you going to tell her what happened?" Celia asked.

"Oh, no, Celia, never! It would scare her to death if she knew I almost fell off the roof," Mandie replied, quickly standing up. "Look at this dress." She looked down at the clothes she had slept in. "It's ruined and I'm a dirty mess."

"Why don't you take a bath?" Celia asked. "You go first while I find something to wear to church." She turned to go to her bedroom.

"I'll hurry, Celia," Mandie promised. She grabbed her robe from a hanger and went into the bathroom. Snowball followed. He liked to play in water, but this morning Mandie shut the door behind her before he could get into the bathroom.

After bathing Mandie felt much better. She also

washed her long blonde hair and briskly rubbed it with a heavy towel to get it dry. She looked at her hands. The water had cleansed most of the scratches and she decided no one would notice. The only thing that really bothered her was the bruise the rope had made on one side of her waist.

"I'll have to wear something that isn't too tight," she told Celia as they got dressed. She took down a yellow silk dress with cream-colored lace trimming. "This dress is a little too big. It ought to be loose enough."

Celia had also bathed and was putting on a pea green silk dress with pink and white rosettes around the high neckline.

"Mandie, I'm sorry you got hurt," Celia told her.

Mandie fastened the buttons up the front of her dress and said, "Celia, it was all my fault for being so stupid. I shouldn't have ever gone out on that roof. I know better, but I just don't know where my brain has been these last few days."

There was a knock on the door. The girls looked anxiously at each other for a moment, wondering who it might be.

"I'll get it," Celia said. "It's probably Jonathan." She went to open the door to the hallway.

"Good morning, miss," Helga greeted her from the hallway. "I came to wake you young ladies for breakfast, but I see you're already up. The meal will be on the table in thirty minutes."

"Thank you," Celia said. Helga turned to go and she closed the door.

Mandie called out from the bedroom, "If you're all ready for breakfast, why don't you see if Jonathan's up while I finish? We could go to the little parlor and talk a few minutes."

"All right," Celia replied and went out the door.

She was back in a couple of minutes. "He's already up and dressed too. He's going down to the parlor to wait for us."

"I'm ready. Let's go," Mandie said, taking a quick glance in the mirror. Her hair was still damp, but it would be dry by the time they left for church. In the meantime, she left it hanging loose. She shut Snowball up in her bedroom.

The three young people discussed the events of the night before as they sat in the parlor. Everyone tried to talk at once.

"Mandie," Jonathan said, "I'll never forgive myself for getting you involved in such a dangerous plan. Just think what could have happened."

Mandie could see the sad expression on his face, and thought she could see a faint trace of tears in his eyes. It made her own blue eyes watery. She had to look away to control herself.

"It wasn't your fault any more than it was mine, Jonathan," she said. "I should have had better sense." Then looking up at Jonathan from where she sat on the settee, she added, "But I am sorry I caused all that trouble—and we still weren't able to get to the tower."

"I think we'd better forget about that tower, Mandie," Celia said. "I was almost scared to death when I saw you fall off the roof. I couldn't even move for a moment. Then all I could think of was that I had to rush up there and help save you."

"Celia, you'll never know how much I love you for

that," Mandie said. "You are a true friend indeed to risk your life for me." Mandie reached out to squeeze Celia's hand. "You were so brave."

"Bravery had nothing to do with it, Mandie," Celia said, returning Mandie's squeeze. "It was a case of fright with the thought that something must be done fast or it'd be too late. After I got to bed last night, the impact of what I had done hit me. I even dreamed about it."

Jonathan spoke up. "Now that we've all patted each other on the back, I think we'd better get on down to breakfast before we're late."

"Oh, Jonathan," Mandie interjected, "I heard that singing again last night. It woke me sometime in the middle of the night, but I sure didn't get up to investigate. Did you hear it?"

"No, I didn't," the boy said. "I wish I had, because I'd have tried to track it down."

"I heard it too, Mandie," Celia said. "But I wasn't about to get out of bed and go roaming around in the darkness."

As they started to leave the room, Mandie said, "I think I heard Uncle Ned come in before we went upstairs last night."

Jonathan opened the door. "I'm just glad he didn't come back while we were getting you back to the roof."

"He would have told my grandmother everything," Mandie agreed. "But on the other hand, he would have saved me from falling.

"And, Jonathan, I've already told Celia that I am not telling my grandmother anything about last night. It would upset her something awful. I learned my lesson and there's no reason to worry her. Please don't say a thing about it."

"Whatever you say," the boy agreed as they went on down the staircase.

When they entered the small dining room where breakfast was served, Uncle Ned was sitting there at the table with Mrs. Taft and Senator Morton. Mandie sat down next to him after everyone exchanged "good mornings."

"Did I hear you come back last night a little before ten o'clock, Uncle Ned?" Mandie said, smiling at the old Cherokee. "You promised to be back by sunset."

"Friends of friends talk late," the old man replied. "Horse throw shoe near village. I get blacksmithy to fix. I get here almost ten o'clock."

"The blacksmith!" Mandie exclaimed. "We met the blacksmith yesterday when we went into the village. He's an Irishman with some strange beliefs." She told him about her conversation with the man while everyone at the table listened.

"Some Cherokee think things like that," the old man told her as they continued to eat. "Some Cherokee need eddicating."

Mandie laughed and reached for Uncle Ned's hand. She immediately realized she shouldn't have done this, because he looked down at her hand and saw the cuts and bruises on the palm. He didn't say anything, but he gave Mandie a questioning look. Mandie quickly withdrew her hand and changed the subject.

"I guess I'd better finish eating so we can get ready for church," Mandie said, with a secret glance at Celia, who had noticed what happened.

"Yes, and don't forget to dress warmly. Those stone benches are cold," Mrs. Taft reminded the young people.

After the meal, Senator Morton went to the stables to get the pony cart ready. He brought it around to the front to pick everyone up.

When they arrived at the church later that morning, the building was almost full, even though they were early. The minister evidently had not arrived, and the local people stole glances at Mandie and her group as they sat down near the door on the last bench. Mandie noticed that Uncle Ned had worn his deerskin jacket, just as he usually did, and had not put on a suit and tie as he had done at the White House when they visited President McKinley earlier that year.

These people have probably never seen an Indian, Mandie thought as she looked about. *Uncle Ned must be the one they are staring at.*

The minister entered from the small door near the altar and he immediately spotted the visitors. He gave them a pleasant smile. He led the group in song. Even though it was in French, the girls managed to hum along. But when he began his sermon in French, Mandie sighed. Jonathan was listening and she would have to ask him later what the man was talking about. Mrs. Taft and Senator Morton could also understand, but she and Celia just looked at each other and smiled.

Mandie's attention wandered during the service and she spotted the blacksmith on a bench in front. She'd like a chance to talk to that man again, but she knew her grandmother would be in a hurry to return to the chalet for the midday meal.

To everyone's surprise, the minister suddenly began speaking in English near the end of his sermon.

"We are greatly honored to have guests today and

we hope that you will come back," he said, looking directly at Mrs. Taft and the senator. "This is a most unusual occasion, because we are so isolated from tourists here. We pray the Lord will bless you and give you a safe return to your home."

Mandie looked down the row and saw her grandmother smiling and nodding as the man spoke.

When the pastor finished his message, the worshipers rose to leave. The minister practically ran to get to Mrs. Taft and shake her hand. Amid the commotion of people moving about, Mandie couldn't hear what her grandmother and the preacher said, but she did see her grandmother reach into her bag and hand the man a piece of paper that looked like a check.

The minister kissed Mrs. Taft's hand and quickly moved along to shake the hands of each person in their group.

When they returned to the chalet, Senator Morton let them out at the front door and took the pony cart on to the stables. Mandie caught a glimpse of the Bagatelles hurrying around behind the chalet with their photographic equipment.

"They're going to take more pictures," Mandie whispered to Jonathan and Celia as they walked behind Mrs. Taft and Uncle Ned toward the front door.

Evidently her grandmother had seen them too. "Those are the most ill-bred people I have ever met up with," Mrs. Taft said. "Never even courteous enough to come to the dinner table."

"Grandmother, could we just look and see where those people are going?" Mandie asked.

"Amanda! You will do no such thing," Mrs. Taft replied. "You will get upstairs and get freshened up and be back down here in fifteen minutes to eat. We'll all meet in the main parlor."

The young people raced up the front steps ahead of Mrs. Taft and Uncle Ned and quickly went to their suites. The girls removed their bonnets, put away their shawls, and touched up their hair while Jonathan went to his suite to wash up.

Snowball was prowling around the suite and Mandie bent down to pet his head. "As soon as we eat I'll take you outside, Snowball," she told the kitten. Snowball meowed and looked up at his mistress.

"That is one way to get outside and see what those people are doing, if they're still out there when we finish eating," Mandie said to Celia.

"I really need some fresh air and a long walk anyway," Celia replied, straightening her long skirt.

The noon meal was soon over because Mrs. Taft had decided she would take a quick nap and then walk in the gardens. The young people were delighted when she gave them permission to go outside. Uncle Ned and the senator were going to sit together in the parlor.

The three young people rushed around the chalet to look for the Bagatelles, but they weren't in sight.

"Let's look down by the pool," Mandie suggested. Snowball was tugging on his leash.

They did not find the Bagatelles, but as the young people started back toward the chalet, they spotted the couple at the front door of the vacant cottage.

The three stepped behind some bushes in order to keep from being seen.

"That's the direction they were looking from the servant's room upstairs. I wonder if they were looking at that cottage," Mandie said excitedly.

"It looks to me like they're trying to get the front door open," Jonathan said.

"I don't see their camera," Celia remarked.

At that moment Snowball managed to pull the leash from Mandie's hand and bound off in the direction of the cottage. Mandie called out and ran after him. The Bagatelles turned and saw her. They quickly walked away from the cottage and the young people saw them retrieve their equipment from the nearby bushes.

Mandie finally caught the kitten in front of the cottage. Jonathan and Celia caught up with her a moment later.

The couple disappeared through the shrubbery. "You know, I wish the Thalers would come home, because I think those people are up to no good," Mandie remarked.

"I agree," Celia said.

"I have an idea—not a dangerous one this time," Jonathan said. "Why don't we watch them until we know they will be busy for a little while, and then we could go upstairs and search their suite."

"Search their rooms? For what?" Mandie asked.

"There might be something there that would give us a clue to their strange behavior, and we might be doing the Thalers a favor if we found these people were doing something wrong," Jonathan explained.

"All right, but we'll have to do this in the daylight," Mandie said. "It's too easy for someone to slip up on us in the dark. Besides, after dark we'd have to turn on lights to see inside their rooms and someone might see that."

"All right, let's find out if they're in their rooms right now," Jonathan suggested.

They hurried back into the house and up the stairs. They listened outside the door of the Bagatelles' suite and could hear them inside.

"All we have to do is sit in the parlor at the top of the steps and watch for them to go by," Mandie whispered to her friends. She led them back down the hall and they entered the small parlor.

"I hope we don't have to wait long, Mandie," Celia remarked, "or your grandmother will be up from her nap and will come right by here looking for us."

"The Begatelles probably won't stay in their rooms long," Jonathan predicted.

The young people sat down to watch and wait.

Chapter 11 / One Mystery Solved

Mandie and her friends sat in the small parlor until tea time. Then Mrs. Taft came by on the way downstairs from her nap. The Bagatelles had not shown up.

"Time for tea," Mrs. Taft remarked as she passed the open door and saw the three sitting in the parlor.

"Yes, Grandmother," Mandie said, and the young people reluctantly rose and followed the lady downstairs.

After having tea, Mrs. Taft insisted they all go for a walk around the grounds. Before long it was time for the evening meal and they hadn't been able to accomplish a thing.

"I think since it's Sunday we should all sit and talk in the parlor for a while before we go to bed," Mrs. Taft said at the table that night.

The three were itching to get away from the adults and check on the Bagatelles, whom they had not seen since noon. But Mrs. Taft kept them in the parlor until she said it was time to retire for the night.

"Well, maybe we can do something tomorrow." Mandie sighed as the three went up the stairs for the night.

Mandie and Celia fell asleep quickly, still tired from their adventure the previous night. Sometime during the night, Mandie woke and heard the singing. She sat up to listen just as Celia did.

"There's the singing. Let's let Jonathan know," Mandie whispered to her friend as she jumped out of bed and grabbed her robe.

Celia followed and put hers on too. "All right," she agreed.

Mandie led the way and quietly opened the door into the hall. They tiptoed over to Jonathan's door and lightly knocked on it. There was only a dim light illuminating the long, dark hallway.

Not receiving any answer Mandie knocked again and again, harder and harder. Finally Jonathan opened the door. At the same time, Uncle Ned opened his door next to Mandie's suite.

"What is it?" Jonathan asked sleepily.

"Papoose, something wrong?" Uncle Ned asked as he stepped into the hall.

Mandie was confused at the sudden development and she stuttered as she tried to answer. "N-Nothing's wrong, Uncle Ned. We just wanted Jonathan to hear the singing," she tried to explain. "Do you hear it?"

She paused and everyone listened intently for a moment, but there was not a sound to be heard.

Mandie and Celia looked at each other. "I know I

heard singing, didn't you, Celia?" Mandie asked.

"Yes, I did. There was definitely someone singing," Celia assured her.

"Singing?" the old Indian questioned them.

The young people stood there in the dark hallway and tried to explain to Uncle Ned about the singing. But when Mandie said there was a rumor that it was the voice of a young girl long dead, Uncle Ned held up his hand to interrupt.

"If girl dead, then she dead. Cannot be here and dead too," the old man said.

"But we don't really believe the tale, Uncle Ned," Mandie told him. "We've been trying to find out what's going on. It has to be something human. I don't believe in ghosts either."

"Evidently it has stopped," Jonathan said. With a big yawn, he said, "I'm going back to bed."

"Yes, we all go to bed," Uncle Ned said, turning to go back to his room. Jonathan closed his door and the girls returned to their suite.

The next day was Monday and the young people knew their visit would end soon, but they had not solved any part of the mystery. They stayed on the lookout for the Bagatelles between meals and walks with the adults.

After supper that night they sat in the parlor while the adults were downstairs. Snowball was allowed to run loose in the room and Mandie kept an eye on him to be sure he didn't decide to leave the room and run down the hallway.

Suddenly she saw him prick up his ears and stand still to stare at the open doorway.

"Snowball hears something," Mandie whispered to her friends.

They watched and waited. In a couple of minutes the Bagatelles came hurrying by and went down the main staircase. The three jumped up.

"At last!" Mandie exclaimed. She listened to make sure that the couple was definitely not returning. From the hallway, she heard them reach the bottom of the steps and hurry out the front door.

"Now's our chance to get into their suite," Jonathan told the girls as he hurried out into the hallway in the direction of the Bagatelles' suite.

The girls followed, Mandie carrying Snowball. Jonathan tried the doorknob—it was unlocked. The three paused in the doorway to survey the room inside. There were no personal belongings in sight; everything was neat and in order. They crept inside and looked into the bedroom. It was the same there. You'd never know anyone was using the suite.

"Where are all their things?" Mandie asked as they looked around. "They brought so much luggage, the two of them could hardly carry it, remember?"

Jonathan turned back the coverlet and examined the sheets.

"Looks like they have been sleeping in the bed. The sheets are rumpled," he said, replacing the covers.

"I hear somebody!" Celia exclaimed and the three quickly darted back into the hallway and closed the door behind them.

There was no one in sight, but as they started back down the corridor to the parlor, the Bagatelles came into sight around the corner. The three smiled at the couple as they passed, but the strangers totally ignored them as they hurried on to their suite.

"Whew! That was a close call!" Mandie said, collapsing on the settee in the parlor. She let Snowball jump back onto the floor.

"I'll say!" Jonathan agreed.

"I'm sure glad they didn't catch us," Celia remarked.

"Now we have another mystery. Where are their belongings? And why don't they keep things in their suite?" Mandie said.

"There is definitely something wrong somewhere," Jonathan said.

"And the only way we can solve this is to search every room in the house," Mandie said. "Their belongings have to be somewhere. We could just follow them around everywhere they go to find out where they are keeping their things."

"That would be next to impossible," Jonathan said. "They'd realize sooner or later that we were watching them. I suppose we'll just have to search for their things."

The girls agreed. But they knew it was time to retire for the night. The search would have to wait until the next day.

As they parted to go to their rooms, Jonathan reminded the girls, "If you hear that singing again, please let me know. Good night."

The girls promised to wake him. However that night there was no singing. Mandie and Celia lay awake into the wee hours of the morning listening for it, but there was not a sound.

The next day the young people did solve one mystery. They were walking around in the gardens when they saw the gardener nearby with a dog on a leash.

Snowball was on his leash and he spit and huffed as the dog came nearer. Mandie tried to pick him up, but he tried to scratch her.

"Snowball! Stop that!" Mandie told the kitten.

When the man was near enough to speak, his dog tried to lunge at Snowball.

Mandie spoke harshly to the man, "Would you please take your dog somewhere else? He's disturbing my cat."

"My dog is the watch dog for the estate," the man told her. "He is allowed to go anywhere. I even take him through the halls of the house late at night to be sure everything is all right." He pulled on the dog's leash.

The three young people looked at each other. Mandie said, "Through the hallways in the house? Did you by any chance bring him down the corridor where we're staying, the night we got here?"

"That I did," the man said. "I open all vacant rooms and check all the halls every night. I did not know you had arrived that night." He walked away with his dog.

"Well, Celia, that settles one mystery," Mandie said. "It was his dog in the hallway that Snowball heard." She held tightly to Snowball's leash as he stared at the departing dog.

"And he turned the doorknob," Celia said.

"Do you suppose he could have anything to do with the singing we hear at night?" Mandie asked her friends.

"I doubt it," said Celia. "I'm sure it's a woman I hear singing."

"That's right," Mandie agreed. "But I thought maybe he might know something about it."

"I don't think it would do any good to ask him. He's

not very friendly," Jonathan reminded the girls.

Mrs. Taft and Senator Morton had gone for a ride in the pony cart that afternoon and the young people were free to go where they pleased. As they walked past the vacant cottage near the house, they stopped to look at it.

"I don't see anything unusual about this cottage," Mandie remarked. "It's just an old empty house. Why are the Bagatelles interested in it?"

They tried to look through the windows, but curtains blocked their view.

"I sure wish we could find the entrance to the tower," Mandie commented. "Why don't we go upstairs and look around that room in the servants' quarters again?"

"Well, since we don't have anything else to do, I suppose we could," Jonathan agreed.

"We'd better watch out for Helga. She won't like it if she catches us in that part of the house," Celia reminded them.

But there didn't seem to be anyone anywhere in the house. They quietly went up the stairs and down the hallways into the servants' quarters.

Mandie walked up to the door of the room they had been in before and put her hand on the doorknob. She listened, but couldn't hear a sound inside the room. Slowly she turned the knob and pushed the door open. There was no one inside.

The first thing she noticed was that someone had straightened the curtain and pulled it together. They had left it pulled back. "The curtain. Someone has been in here," Mandie remarked as she went to the window and pushed the curtain back. She looked out and gasped.

"Look! There are the Bagatelles down there at that cottage again."

Her friends crowded close to look out. It looked as though the strangers were trying different keys in the lock of the front door in an effort to get it open.

"Do you suppose they could have their luggage hidden in that cottage?" Mandie asked. But she realized how absurd that would be and said, "No, that couldn't be, because they would have a key or some way to open the door."

"Let's go back outside and watch them," Jonathan suggested.

The three hurried quietly through the house and into the yard. They hid behind shrubbery to watch the Bagatelles trying to get the door to the cottage open. Mandie held Snowball in her arms to keep him from interfering as he had the last time.

The couple talked in low voices, but the girls couldn't understand anything they were saying because it was in French. Jonathan whispered, "I can't hear well enough to translate."

The couple finally gave up. The man put the keys in his pocket and they walked back toward the house while Mandie and her friends watched from behind the bushes.

As soon as the Bagatelles were out of sight, Mandie said, "Come on. Let's see if anything's different." She led the way to the front door of the cottage.

"I don't see anything different," Jonathan said, looking around.

"There is something about this cottage that interests the Bagatelles," Mandie muttered as she looked around.

"They always seem to be trying to get inside," Celia remarked.

"We know the Bagatelles' photographic equipment wasn't in their suite," Jonathan said. "Maybe they have it locked up in here."

"But remember," said Mandie, "if they locked something up in this cottage they would have a key to unlock the door, wouldn't they? It looked to me like the man had a handful of keys and was trying each one to get the door unlocked."

"Is there no back door?" Celia asked.

The three looked at each other and Mandie laughed. "We haven't even looked for another door. Come on." She led the way around the cottage.

The back of the house was hidden with thick shrubbery. They squeezed through it and Mandie exclaimed, "Celia, there is another door." A crossbar on the outside held it shut.

"Let's see if it'll open," Mandie said, trying to lift the bar.

Jonathan and Celia helped. But when they got the bar off and tried the door, they found it securely locked. They replaced the bar and tried peeping through the back windows, but curtains kept them from seeing anything inside.

"If that doesn't beat all!" Mandie exclaimed. "It sure is locked up tight for an empty house."

As they walked around the cottage, Eckart came down the path. They had not felt comfortable asking Eckart about anything since he wouldn't tell them what he knew about the tower. Nevertheless, he stopped and spoke. "I hope you are enjoying your visit here," he said politely as he looked from one to the other.

"Yes, we are, Eckart," Mandie told him. "We were just curious about this cottage. You told us it was vacant, didn't you?"

"Yes, it is, miss," Eckart replied. "It has not been occupied since the Thalers came here."

"It's all locked up. Do you have a key for it? We'd like to see inside," Mandie told him.

"No, only Hedgewick has keys. You could ask her," Eckart said.

Mandie thanked him and he went on his way.

"I don't think I want to go ask Mrs. Hedgewick to unlock this cottage for us, do you?" Mandie asked her friends.

"No, she'd probably be awfully suspicious of us and she'd outright refuse," Jonathan said.

"Well, I suppose we could go back to the house and see where the Bagatelles went," Mandie decided.

They didn't find the Bagatelles for the rest of the day, even though they looked for the couple wherever they went.

Disappointed that they seemed no closer to solving the mystery of the tower or the cottage, the young people went to bed that night feeling that they had not accomplished anything more than discovering who was walking through their hallway late at night.

Mandie and Celia were fast asleep that night when Mandie was again awakened by singing. She punched Celia, and said, "I hear singing."

She quickly jumped out of bed and grabbed her robe.

Celia blinked her eyes, but was out of bed in just a

moment putting on her robe. She followed Mandie out into the hallway where Mandie was already knocking on Jonathan's door.

This time Jonathan heard the first knock. He came to the door fully dressed.

"Listen, there's that singing!" Mandie whispered.

"I heard it too," Jonathan said. "I got dressed so I could take a look. Come on. Let's investigate."

"It's a lot fainter than it has been," Celia remarked as they tried to figure out what direction to go.

"I think it's coming from the yard this time," Mandie said. "Just like Celia said before." They quietly hurried down the hallway to the top of the main staircase.

No one noticed, but Snowball had followed his mistress. When they went down the steps, he went too.

Pausing in the front hallway, Mandie said, "It must be coming from behind the house. You notice how faint it is here."

"Right," whispered Jonathan.

They stealthily unlocked the front door and stepped outside. As they crept around the house in the darkness, Snowball stayed right with them.

"The tower?" Mandie asked, and they stopped to look up at the tall section of the house.

"No," Jonathan said, shaking his head.

"The cottage!" Celia whispered.

"Yes, yes," Mandie and Jonathan said together as the three excitedly rushed toward the vacant cottage.

Sure enough, the singing grew louder as they approached the little house. They stopped right in front of it, hiding behind a shrub in case anyone could see them.

"Someone is inside there singing," Mandie whispered. Jonathan and Celia nodded, for there was no question about where the beautiful voice was coming from.

The three began to creep closer. But they stopped suddenly when they heard footsteps running toward them. The Bagatelles came hurrying to the cottage and began pounding on the front door. The singing immediately stopped.

The three young people caught their breath in alarm as they watched. Mr. Bagatelle picked up a rock and knocked out a small glass pane in one of the windows. Mrs. Bagatelle continued knocking and shaking the door.

Mandie gasped as Snowball bounced out of the bushes in front of her and went straight for the Bagatelles. He meowed and beat at the man's pants legs with his paws.

Mandie screamed as the man tried to kick Snowball. She rushed forward and snatched up her kitten.

"Don't you dare kick my cat!" she told the man angrily.

The man and woman took one look at Mandie and turned to rush off toward the chalet. But Jonathan put out his foot and tripped the man as the couple came past the bushes where he and Celia were still hiding. The man yelled at Jonathan as he got up and brushed off his clothes.

"That's what you get for kicking an innocent animal," Jonathan said to the man in English.

"Just you wait!" the man yelled back as he and the woman continued on toward the house.

Mandie and her friends rushed up to the cottage to

investigate. They tried to see through the broken windowpane, but the only thing visible was the inside wall.

Mandie knocked on the door and called out, "I don't know who you are but we're your friends. Won't you please open the door and let us in?"

There was complete silence inside.

"The bad people are gone. We want to help you," Celia said through the broken windowpane.

"Please open the door," Jonathan said.

There was no response of any kind. The three young people looked at each other in puzzlement.

"There has to be somebody in there," Mandie said. "And whoever it is was the person we heard singing."

"And for some reason the Bagatelles were trying to break in," Jonathan added.

"Why don't we go for help? We could get Mrs. Hedgewick to unlock the door," Celia suggested.

"No, not Mrs. Hedgewick," Mandie said. "Uncle Ned! He'll know what to do. I'll go get him. Y'all stay here and watch to be sure whoever it is doesn't leave without us seeing them."

Jonathan and Celia agreed. Mandie put her kitten down so she could run faster. "Snowball, you stay here," she told him.

She ran off toward the house. Uncle Ned always knew how to solve problems. He would know what to do about whoever was in the cottage.

Chapter 12 / The Tales Explained

Mandie knocked hard on Uncle Ned's door. "Uncle Ned, please come quick! We need you!"

When the old man opened the door, he was fully dressed. He looked at Mandie in alarm. "Papoose! What?"

"There's someone in the cottage and we can't get her out," Mandie told him incoherently. She took his hand. "Please come with me."

The old Indian allowed Mandie to lead him down the stairs and around to the cottage. She practically ran all the way.

Uncle Ned kept asking, "What wrong, Papoose?"

Mandie kept saying, "Wait. You'll see."

When they finally got to the cottage, Mandie was out of breath and Jonathan explained to the old man about what the Bagatelles had done and that there was someone inside.

"Maybe someone live here," Uncle Ned said, as they stood in front of the cottage.

"No, Uncle Ned. Eckart said this cottage was empty," Mandie told him. "Besides, I forgot to tell you, the singing we heard was coming from inside this house tonight."

The old Indian looked puzzled. "Cannot break into someone's house," he told the young people.

"But nobody lives here," Mandie argued. "It's not anybody's house."

"House belong Thalers," Uncle Ned emphatically told her. "Not mine, not yours."

"I know, Uncle Ned, but the Thalers are not here and someone is in there," Mandie said. "I know it must be a woman because we heard her singing."

"Knock," the old Indian told her.

"We did, but I'll try it again," Mandie replied. She lifted her hand and knocked hard on the door.

Everyone listened. There was no sound inside. Snowball jumped up on a railing nearby, took one look at his mistress, and jumped through the broken window. Mandie gasped.

"Now Snowball has got inside!" Mandie said. "How am I going to get him out?" She bent in front of the broken glass and called to him. "Snowball, come back here."

Jonathan had been listening. Now he spoke up. "There is someone inside, Uncle Ned. Whoever it is won't answer. Maybe they are ill or hurt or something."

Uncle Ned looked around. "No way to get in," he said.

"We haven't tried the windows," Jonathan said.

"There could be one that's unlocked."

They quickly examined the few windows in the house. Every one was securely locked.

Mandie came back to the broken pane and once more called to her kitten. "Snowball, please come here. Kitty, kitty, kitty."

Suddenly she heard movement inside the cottage. She looked up and saw Snowball being pushed through the broken window.

"Your cat, you take," said a voice inside.

Everyone crowded around to look as Mandie reached for Snowball. A tiny old woman was handing him up to her.

"Are you all right?" Mandie asked. She took Snowball and tried to look inside. It was dark and there were no lights in the cottage.

"That man and woman tried to catch me. He lost the key. I found it," the woman explained. "I hide in here and lock the door. He can't get in."

"The Bagatelles?" Mandie asked, excitedly. "What did they chase you for?"

"I sing," the woman said.

"I know. We heard you sing," Mandie replied. "Do you live in here?"

"No, no, I live on the mountain," the woman said. "Good night now. I must get some rest." She moved out of Mandie's sight.

"Wait, please don't go," Mandie said quickly. "Open the door and let us in, please. We want to help you."

"This is my dressing room. I must get some rest before I go on stage," the woman mumbled from further back inside the house.

Everyone looked at each other. Who was this woman talking about a dressing room and a stage?

"I don't think she's just right," Jonathan said.

Uncle Ned looked at the young people and said, "Lady live in old times maybe."

"Old times?" Celia questioned.

"The past," Mandie said, understanding what the old man meant. "The lady is living in her memories I suppose."

"How are we going to get her out?" Jonathan asked.

"She said she had to rest before she goes on stage," Celia said. "Maybe she'll just come out after she rests."

"You may be right, Celia," Mandie said. She bent in front of the broken window and called, "It's time to go on stage. Are you ready?"

The old lady immediately came back to the window and said, "Yes, dear, I'll be right there." She disappeared again.

Everyone waited and watched silently. In a minute they heard a key turn in the lock on the inside. The door was opened and a tiny old woman came out of the cottage wearing an old-fashioned formal gown. Her gray hair hung loose down below her waist.

As they watched, the woman spread the skirt of her gown in a curtsy and smiled at them. She suddenly ran as fast as she could in the direction of the chalet. They followed her.

She went directly to the stone patio at the back of the house and stopped in the center of it. After she had turned around to face them, the night air was suddenly filled with operatic singing. She didn't falter over a single note. Mandie and her friends stood there and watched in wonderment as the lady performed.

Suddenly the singing stopped and the lady curtsied again. Everyone automatically applauded. The woman smiled and threw kisses. Jonathan on impulse snatched a bloom from the garden where they were standing and ran forward to present it to the lady. She took it with a big smile and curtsied and they applauded.

Once again, she began singing.

By this time, Mrs. Taft and Senator Morton had heard the commotion. After they found the young people missing from their rooms, they had come outside to see what was going on.

"Amanda!" Mrs. Taft called to her granddaughter as she approached. "What is going on?"

"Grandmother! Listen! Isn't she wonderful!" Mandie replied, clapping as the woman finished singing.

"Who is this woman?" Senator Morton asked Uncle Ned.

"Was locked in little house," the old Indian said, pointing to the cottage below.

Mrs. Taft walked closer to get a better look at the woman in the bright moonlight. "What is your name?" she asked.

"I am Maria Zaranova! I am known around the world for my voice," the woman said emphatically. "I must go home now."

The woman started to walk away, but Mandie quickly grasped her hand and asked, "Why don't you come inside the big house with us? We could talk a little."

"I must conserve my voice and get my rest for to-morrow night's performance," the woman said. "In between shows I will visit with you, dear."

Mrs. Taft spoke to the senator. "Do you think she could really be Maria Zaranova?" she asked.

Senator Morton thought for a moment and said, "I don't believe I remember what happened to Maria Zaranova after she disappeared from the world of opera. Yes, this lady could possibly be her."

Mrs. Taft stopped the woman as she was leaving and asked several questions about operas and theaters that Mandie's grandmother was knowledgeable about. The woman evidently gave the correct answers, for Mrs. Taft turned back to everyone and said, "This really must be Maria Zaranova. She knew the answer to everything I asked. I can remember going to the opera with my parents when I was a tiny girl to hear her sing. She was the world's greatest."

The young people were excited. They gathered around the woman who stood there smiling at them.

"You mean she really is a famous opera star?" Mandie asked.

"She used to be the most important singer of her day," Mrs. Taft said. "And I can't remember what happened to her, but here she is, as sure as I'm alive."

"Where do you live now, Miss Zaranova?" Senator Morton asked the lady.

"Up on the mountain—that way," Miss Zaranova said, pointing off to her left. "I have to come down to the theater every night, every night except Monday. You know the theater is always closed on Monday, and I get an extra day's rest then."

The senator looked at Mrs. Taft. "I'm afraid she's still living in the past," he said under his breath.

The woman started to leave again. "I must go home now and get some rest."

Mrs. Taft stepped forward. "But won't you please come into the house and visit with your fans for a moment? We'd love to give you a cup of tea. It would refresh your voice."

The woman thought for a moment and then agreed. "All right, but only for a moment. Let's hurry now."

They all walked around the house and in through the front door. Mrs. Hedgewick was dressed and standing inside the hallway when Mandie marched in carrying Snowball.

"I heard such a commotion. Is something wrong, madam?" she asked.

"Not really, Mrs. Hedgewick," Mrs. Taft said. Turning to the others she said, "Would y'all please take Miss Zaranova into the parlor and I'll see to ordering tea."

As they moved on toward the parlor, Mandie lingered behind to hear what her grandmother said to the housekeeper. Mrs. Hedgewick was plainly shocked. She could hardly believe such a thing had happened.

"This solves the mystery of the tower being haunted by the singing young woman, Mrs. Hedgewick. Aren't you glad?" Mandie said.

"Why, yes, dear. Mr. and Mrs. Thaler will be well pleased to have that tale settled," Mrs. Hedgewick said. "Now I will see to tea if you can keep the lady occupied." She disappeared down the hallway.

"Imagine this," said Mrs. Taft as she walked with Mandie to the parlor, "imagine having tea at this hour of the night, or morning I should say. I do believe it's after midnight."

Mrs. Taft went on inside and sat down near Maria Zaranova. Mandie motioned to her friends to come outside into the hallway. The three walked back to the main staircase at the front door and sat on the steps.

"Where do you suppose the Bagatelles went?" Mandie asked, softly.

"Probably back to their suite," Celia said.

"I doubt that. They know we caught them doing something they weren't supposed to be doing. I wonder who they really are anyway," Jonathan remarked.

"They must be gangsters, or half-crazy people, or something like that to be acting the way they have," Mandie said. Snowball squirmed in her arms and she put him down.

"Isn't it wonderful that we found a long-lost opera star?" Celia said.

"And that we solved the mystery of the 'haunted' tower with the singing myth?" Mandie added. "But there is one mystery we haven't been able to solve: Where is the entrance to the tower?"

Snowball had disappeared and Mandie quickly looked around for him. She and her friends walked back toward a door under the main staircase. It was open a crack.

"Oh, he went in there!" said Mandie, pointing at the secluded door. She rushed over to open the door and exclaimed, "This must be the door to the cellar."

Someone seemed to be holding the door on the inside and Mandie couldn't pull it open. It wasn't locked because it moved an inch or two when she tried it.

"Who's in there?" Mandie demanded as she tried to pull the door open.

Jonathan and Celia stepped forward to help, and when the three gave a hard jerk, the door flew open.

There to their amazement was the strange woman from the ship who had been mysteriously following them everywhere they went in Europe. They stood there petrified, staring at the woman.

"The Bagatelles have packed and gone," the woman said quickly, and she thrust some papers at Mandie. "Read these. You'll understand."

Mandie took the papers and her friends crowded around. Without their noticing, the woman quickly left the house.

"Look at this!" Mandie said, holding out a single sheet of the paper. "Those people were reporters for a magazine. This is a letter giving them the assignment to investigate the rumors of singing at this house. Of all the nerve, pretending to be friends of the Thalers."

Jonathan and Celia quickly read it. "And the editor wrote the note that was supposed to have been from the Thalers inviting them to come visit. They knew all the time the Thalers were gone and they picked this time to get into the house."

"This is some kind of a diary they'd been keeping," Mandie said, showing them a small notebook in the stack of papers. "Look at that. They wrote here that they were planning to lock the lady up somewhere so everyone would still think the tower was haunted. They didn't want anyone to see her because they wanted to write about how mysterious the singing was."

"I knew there was something wrong about those people," Jonathan said while he and Celia were looking over the notebook.

Suddenly Mandie said, "In all the excitement, I've forgotten Snowball!" She turned around and went back to see where the kitten had run off to.

She opened the door with Jonathan and Celia behind her and the three gasped. "The stairs to the tower!" the three cried together as they surveyed the narrow, winding staircase that went all the way up, out of sight.

"Come on!" Mandie said to her friends as she led the way.

By the time they got to the top their legs were rubbery. "Look!" she cried as she came to a room at the top, "this is the tower room!"

Her friends joined her. They looked around the stone-walled room. There was nothing there, not a single piece of furniture except for an old wooden crate sitting by one of the windows. Mandie quickly examined the curtains.

"The curtains are clean. I told y'all," she said. "Someone has been keeping the curtains clean."

They looked out the windows and could see all the way to the Alps.

Suddenly there was a loud meow, and Mandie looked around to find Snowball sitting on a high ledge near a window. "I'm sorry I forgot all about you, Snowball," Mandie ran to rescue him.

"Mandie, I think we'd better go back downstairs," Celia said. "Your grandmother is going to wonder where we are."

"You're right. Let's go. I want to talk to Miss Zaranova anyway," Mandie said.

The three young people and Snowball went back down the stairs faster than they had come up, even though it was dark in the windowless stairwell.

When they arrived at the bottom, the door was shut.

Trying to open it, Jonathan discovered it was locked. "Someone locked the door," Jonathan announced.

"Now what?" Mandie said, picking up Snowball so he wouldn't run away again.

"Let's knock real hard. Someone will hear us, I'm sure," Celia said.

The three of them knocked hard for a few minutes, but they thought no one had heard. Then a key turned in the door and Mrs. Hedgewick stood there in the doorway.

"Where have you been?" she asked sternly.

"We're sorry, Mrs. Hedgewick," Mandie apologized. "You see, a woman we sorta know came out of here and left the door open. We found out the stairs led to the tower so that's where we've been."

"You should not have gone up those steps. They are in dangerous condition. The foundation is cracking," Mrs. Hedgewick reprimanded them. She looked at the girls' nightclothes. "Don't you young ladies think you ought to go dress or go back to bed now?"

Mandie and Celia suddenly realized they had been running around in their nightclothes. Jonathan laughed as they walked out into the hallway. Mrs. Hedgewick locked the door behind them.

"Come to think of it, my grandmother and Senator Morton were dressed when they came out of the house a while ago," Mandie said. "We're the only ones running around half-dressed."

"What shall we do?" Celia asked.

"Oh, well, since everyone has already seen us this way, we might as well go on into the parlor," Mandie decided. She still held on to Snowball and the papers the woman had given her as she led the way to the parlor.

Mrs. Taft, Senator Morton and Uncle Ned were sitting near Miss Zaranova, evidently having an interesting visit with her. When the young people entered the room, the woman stood up and said, "My, my, here are my fans. You almost missed me, dears. I must be going home now."

Uncle Ned stood up and said, "I take lady home. I see where she live."

"Would you please, Uncle Ned?" Mrs. Taft said. "Now that we've found her, we don't want to lose her."

"Grandmother, please let me go too," Mandie begged.

"And me," Jonathan said.

"And me, too," Celia said.

"All right, I suppose since we're all up and around it'll be all right," Mrs. Taft replied. "But, Amanda and Celia, you must get dressed—and quickly—this lady won't wait much longer."

The girls rushed upstairs, dressed, and returned as fast as they could. Mrs. Taft had made arrangements with Mrs. Hedgewick for Uncle Ned to use the pony cart.

Miss Zaranova showed them the way over rough trails and through thickets that the pony and cart could barely get through. At last they came within sight of a tiny shack high on the side of a mountain. Then they had to leave the cart and walk the rest of the way up the steep incline.

"You sure do live a long way up the mountain, Miss Zaranova, to come all the way down to the chalet every night," Mandie remarked as they climbed upward.

"Walking is good for the legs, keeps them trim," the lady said.

The young people noticed she didn't seem to be out of breath at all when they reached the hut. She stopped them at the door and turned to say, "I will bid you good night here. I must go inside and get my rest."

Uncle Ned told the woman, "We will see you again."

"Yes, please do," Miss Zaranova replied as she opened the warped door, its rusty hinges squeaking in protest.

The young people got a glimpse inside, seeing only meager furnishings. Then the woman closed the door behind her.

"Oh, she is pitiful," Mandie said with tears in her voice. "We've got to do something to help her."

"Yes, we must share what Big God gives us," Uncle Ned agreed as they started back down hill.

When they arrived back at the house, Mrs. Taft and the senator were still in the parlor waiting for them. After the young people discussed the pitiful plight of the woman, they all decided to do something to help.

"Why, I don't imagine she has enough to eat," Senator Morton said. "She looked thin as a rail."

"She wouldn't have any way to make a living I don't suppose," Mrs. Taft said.

Mandie spoke up. "Grandmother, I want you to give her all my spending money, the cash you are holding for me for this tour of Europe. I don't need it."

"Mine too, Mrs. Taft," Celia volunteered.

"Well, I don't have any right now, but as soon as I can get some money, I'll be glad to do my part too," Jonathan said.

Mrs. Taft looked at the group and smiled. "We'll do something for her before we leave the country."

"When are we leaving Switzerland?" Mandie asked.

"Probably the day after tomorrow," Mrs. Taft said. "I think we've had a nice rest here and it's time to get out and do something."

The young people suddenly remembered the strange woman from the ship, and they all started to tell Mandie's grandmother about her at once. Mrs. Taft sorted out the facts from their conversation and was amazed that the woman had been seen in the Thalers' house and that the Bagatelles had turned out to be reporters.

"I can't imagine how that woman from the ship ever followed us here, nor have I any idea what she wanted," Mrs. Taft said. "And those Bagatelles, I knew there was something wrong with them. They just didn't seem right to me."

Mandie turned to her friend Uncle Ned and asked, "Are you going to Germany with us when we leave here, Uncle Ned?"

"Maybe, Papoose," he said. His old face wrinkled up with a broad smile.

"We're going to visit a real baroness in a real castle there," Mandie told him. "We met her in Italy, you know, and she insisted that Grandmother and all of us come to visit."

"She has a grandson too," Celia added. "And he took us for a ride in their motor car in Italy."

"The Baroness Geissler," Mrs. Taft spoke up. "That's her name."

"Grandmother, is there any mystery connected to her castle?" Mandie asked.

"Not that I know of, dear, but then I've never been there," Mrs. Taft said with a smile.

"I suppose we'll just have to wait and see," Mandie said. Celia and Jonathan both nodded their agreement.